Allan Massie

Allan Massie was born in Singapore in 1938. He is the author of twelve novels, including THE LAST PEACOCK, winner of the Frederick Niven Award in 1981, A QUESTION OF LOYALTIES, winner of the Saltire/*Scotsman* Book of the Year, THE SINS OF THE FATHER, his widely acclaimed Roman novels, AUGUSTUS, TIBERIUS and CAESAR, and his latest, KING DAVID. His non-fiction books include BYRON'S TRAVELS, a biography of Colette and a book on Edinburgh. He also writes regularly for the *Daily Telegraph* and is the lead fiction reviewer for *The Scotsman*. Allan Massie is a Fellow of the Royal Society of Literature and lives in the Scottish Borders.

SCEPTRE

Also by Allan Massie and published by Sceptre

Augustus
Tiberius
Caesar
King David
A Question of Loyalties
The Ragged Lion
The Sins of the Father

These Enchanted Woods

A Comedy of Morals

ALLAN MASSIE

SCEPTRE

First published in Great Britain in 1993 by Hutchinson
First published in paperback in 1994 by Hodder and Stoughton
A division of Hodder Headline PLC
A Sceptre Paperback

10 9 8 7 6 5 4 3 2

A CIP catalogue record for this book is
available from the British Library

ISBN 0 340 60964 8

Printed and bound in Great Britain by
Cox and Wyman Ltd, Reading, Berkshire

Hodder and Stoughton
A division of Hodder Headline PLC
338 Euston Road
London NW1 3BH

For Alison, again.

'Enter these enchanted woods,
    You who dare.'
    George Meredith, *The Woods of Westermain*

I

She stood on the hotel steps in a pale-grey linen suit, the jacket open over a pale-pink shirt (the colour of strawberries mashed with thick cream), regular, white, dentist's-joy teeth nibbling a pale-pink nether lip, and a navy blue shoulder-bag dangling, stood there on thin high heels as if there was no one else in the street. She was, he thought, still like a film star.

Absurd, for she had never been remotely that, had had no aspirations in that direction, unlike, perhaps, her sister Belinda. The sight of her there took him back years. He watched her, thirty yards off, alert, his senses quickening, but something in her attitude, something lost and icy even in that June afternoon with the sun high and no wind, restrained his initial impulse. He had loved her all those years ago. She had been his first love, his true girl-on-a-magazine-cover first love. Seeing her sent calendars rolling. His heart lifted and he felt also regret, even distress, for the years between and what he had made of them and they of him. Coming on her was like those old movies where the girl is unpacking a trunk and finds a dance programme with (of course) a flower pressed in it: a gardenia inevitably. The thought made him smile. Then it came to him: she needed help. The realization held him at a distance.

For she had treated him badly. She had loved him and then looked him over with a calm appraisal he couldn't himself achieve, and foreseen her life with him as a succession of dead evenings in London basement-flats while she awaited his return from work; and had shut him out. She knew what she wanted: possessions and status and no waiting. He couldn't offer that; what he could

1

offer wasn't enough. So she had said no, and zipped up their affair.

He couldn't blame her, not reasonably. But he did, of course, nightly, and for years, as her image flickered before him. Long ago.

She turned away, into a heavy sweep of revolving doors, into the hotel dark. He hovered on the edge of following. But she would have gone, into some recess—marriage, motherhood, an affair—where he couldn't follow, which would render her as remote and inaccessible, as she had been this lost decade and more. As for him, he looked at his wrist watch; he would be late for his appointment.

Fiona had only just managed to get through the committee meeting. But she was good at meetings, and strain had only made her brisker and more efficient even than usual. Her chairmanship was admired; she knew that, without today deriving satisfaction from the knowledge. She was tired. She hadn't been able to eat any of the buffet lunch provided and now longed for tea before driving home. She ordered Lapsang and sat in the lounge. A couple of businessmen eyed her. She felt their gaze drift away as yet again she replayed in her mind Kevin's savage dismissal, the words of rage, contempt and frustration he had thrown at her in his eagerness to bring things to an end.

The hotel surrounded her like those screens they put round hospital beds. Its carelessness and anonymity gave her time. She didn't want to go home, to hear Gavin mutter banalities as he poured himself a gin twice the size of hers, or, more difficult to respond to, to be loved by the children. She wanted out, for the moment, like those characters in soaps who said they needed time to themselves. She didn't yet realize that she herself had willed the end of Kevin, as she saw her mother's way of life seem to spread itself before her.

She crossed to the reception desk, and asked if she might have a room. Then she went over the street to the store where she had a charge account, and bought pyjamas, slippers, a dressing-gown, night cream, underwear, a shirt, trousers, and other shoes for tomorrow.

Back in the hotel, in her room, with the curtain drawn to deny all but a streak of sunlight, she called home, spoke to the nanny, then took a long hot bath.

Tony came into the hotel bar and saw her sitting there with a bottle of Perrier in front of her, and this time couldn't dodge the encounter. He excused himself a moment to the men with him and approached the table. ('That's my Tony, just watch this,' he heard Freddy say, and laugh.)

'Fiona,' he said.

She looked up, big cornflower eyes startled as if she hadn't registered that he spoke her name like an old friend.

'It's me,' he said. 'Tony Lubbock, greying, battered, but me. What a lovely surprise. When I saw you . . .'

Did she really not know him? He sat down. It wasn't possible that she shouldn't. But she looked at him as if they had never slept together. And he still, in night watches, heard the words she used in love-making, could shiver at the remembered tone.

'Extraordinary,' he said, and knew he was prattling, off his stroke, 'extraordinary, haven't been in Scotland for yonks and come up to do a spot of business and walk straight into you.'

But she still had nothing to say, as if he wasn't there.

'I say, are you all right?'

And that got home.

'I'm sorry, I can't, I don't know,' the words fluttered out, and, picking up her bag, she was off. In flight, no question.

'Flea in the ear, Tony,' said the big red-faced lawyer. 'Flea in the ear, old boy.' He wafted his tumbler of malt before him. 'Tell us why you're left with egg on your face, eh?'

3

Telling was a long story he couldn't embark on and so joked away. But telling remained with him all through the dinner. Telling or not telling disturbed the *filet mignon*. Telling, something he wasn't used to, stayed with him till, late at night, the red-faced lawyer departed to his New Town home and Tony was left with Freddy Paynter, old crony, business partner, in deals and girl-chasing, since they had come together in a City wine bar a dozen years ago, both young sparks on the rise, and had recognized an affinity straight away.

'That girl,' Tony said now, 'some brandy? You've been wondering. My first love, my girl-on-a-magazine-cover, you know the song . . .' He let it rest there till the brandy came and he rolled it round like memory in his glass. 'You know, Freddy, old boy, old son, one of the things about us, besides . . . well put it this way . . . we share a lot, don't we? The business, natch, and racing at Sandown and golf and a good few jaunts, Christ we've even shared the same girls before now . . . but, besides that, one thing we have in common, one of the bonds, is that we're both men of today, without pasts or en-cumbrances. We don't go back, do we? Where is it you come from? Chesterfield, Buxton, some place like that? But the point is, it doesn't matter. I suppose you have parents. We never see them, do we? You do, of course, but they don't obtrude. I don't have to know them. And that goes for Irene and Susie. No background, no bloody family connections, no bloody family complications. Christ we're the sort of men that make the old joke about mother-in-laws obsolete. Nothing before adult life exists. That's right, isn't it? Not like that red-faced bugger with his old school tie and reunion dinners and family lunch in Heriot Row every Sunday, or Moray Place, or whatever. You see what I'm getting at, don't you? We've dispensed with all that. Cut it right out. Only of course it can't be quite like that, not really, ever. Buried somewhere we all have pasts.'

'Christ, Tony, some more brandy, I think.'

'And that girl, she's a significant part . . .'

4

But he tailed off. When he came to it, he couldn't. The habit of reticence was too strong. Whatever he had to say wouldn't disturb Freddy. He knew that. Freddy was intelligent. Freddy was a happy man, living in the sunshine of the present, with the villa in Sevenoaks, his Saturday golf, his gin-and-tonic, his poolside barbecues, and their expanding business. It wouldn't disturb him, not much, but he wouldn't like Tony going over the past. Not that sort of past. Recalling their first jaunts to Barcelona, how they'd made their first big deal and picked up clap from the same half-Arab whore the same night, fun memories like that, yes, but he wouldn't know how he was expected to react if Tony invaded his English sense of privacy and went on:

'My name isn't Lubbock, you know. The old man chose Lubbock when he settled in Edinburgh because he thought it had some sort of class, God knows why. But he was born Bukalo. Ukrainian. You can see it in my cheekbones, more clearly every year. Refugee from Stalin. Lucky not to be handed back, I daresay. Built up a nice little grocery business, though he used to talk of having been a lawyer back home. That's what half of them claimed. I wouldn't know. Still he did well enough before the supermarkets came on the scene, well enough to send me to one of the Merchant Company schools. Modest enough fees—by the standard we're paying—but still a tie that carried respect here. I don't wear it of course, but I don't mock it either. It had a good science side. Just the place for the upwardly mobile, and Christ was I mobile by the time I reached the Uni. Saw all sorts of careers open to my talent, before I fell back on money. Acquired well-born friends who introduced me to the County, landed gentry, you know, lairds we call them up here. Turned my Dad into a White Russian, seemed to have a touch more class, and nobody knew a damn thing about Ukrainians. Oh, yes, Freddy old son, I flew high for a couple of years. But now'—he would slap his bulging thigh—'the Ukrainian's coming through. Look at my nose too, that's the real me. But in that false

5

youth'—he could get lyrical here and talk of Spring and apple-blossom—'I met Fiona. And loved her. Loved her like I've loved nobody since. Loved her from a distance even when we made love. Always will love her, one part of me, from a well of fresh love deep inside me, which I would have thought quite dried up. Always will love her. Not like Susie, not at all like my wife.'

That last line wouldn't have shocked Freddy. But the sentiment of undying love might have made him laugh, to cover his embarrassment, made him wonder if his old mate wasn't going soft on him. Still, a little sentiment was permissible, it went with the Remy Martin and the hour. So Tony gave him another version of his first love, lightened by ribaldry, still touched with the sentimental regret that Freddy could respond to; he was English and so moved by autumn melancholy recalling spring.

Tony woke in the middle of the night, aware of her there, in the same hotel, under the same roof. He didn't know her room number of course, didn't even know her married name; the notion of breaking in on her was wild fancy. But he lay there and pictured her, and remembered, and couldn't sleep again.

He looked for her in the breakfast room, but she didn't appear, and there was still no sign of her by the time Freddy hustled him from the foyer (where he had sat for half an hour, giving the *Financial Times* less close attention than usual) for their first meeting of the day.

But on the train south that afternoon, he knew, looking out to the flat sea east of Berwick, that he couldn't just let it go. His pride was challenged. He was thirty-eight; he had just had to instruct his tailor to make the trousers of his new suits a couple of inches wider at the waist. Playing golf the last damp Saturday, he had felt a twinge of what could only be rheumatism, fibrositis, something middle-aged, evidence of departed youth. He looked out to sea: there were no fishing-boats, coasters, tankers, navy vessels. It was quite empty, a waste of blue, disturbed only by the wheeling flocks of gulls. One detached itself from the swirl and dived for a fish.

On the hotel writing-paper Fiona set down her last letter to Kevin. She didn't scold or plead. The time was past. It was all over, a line could be drawn. Should she thank him? But for what? There were no words for the gratitude, the sort of gratitude she perversely still felt. And if she had found words, he wouldn't have realized how discriminating they were. 'I'm not a words person'; how often had he come out with that silly boast. Besides, gratitude was corrupted by the manner in which he had snapped their affair shut, by the relief with which he had freed himself. So she said nothing of that. Instead she asked him to return her letters, care of her solicitor; her personal lawyer, not the firm that handled estate business. She reminded him that they remained her property. She had no letters from him. She had spared herself that embarrassment early on.

Then, before going home, to put it off a little longer, to be for another hour this person who was more fully herself and yet not herself, she walked along Princes Street to the National Gallery. She stood before the great Titians lent by the Duke of Sutherland. Japanese tourists, jeaned students, and once a band of schoolgirls, interposed themselves between her and the canvases, but she saw them all out and continued to gaze on the warm accepting flesh in the foreground, the dark mystery of the woods that fringed the scene, the golden light that suffused all, the crumbling classical order. Her tongue touched her lower lip as she sought the meaning of what Titian offered her. It would have surprised her family to see her there; they never allowed her either the taste or sensibility she possessed. They couldn't be blamed; that was how she had presented herself.

It wasn't till she had edged her Lancia out of the city and had the Ochil Hills in view that she let herself remember Tony Lubbock.

7

II

Bruised-purple clouds hung over the beech trees ahead. To the right of the road sunlight still danced pink and gold on the upper branches of a plantation of Scots Pine. But it was already raining where Fiona was going. She eased her foot off the accelerator. The car was filled with the slow movement of Dvořák's New World: the melancholy sound of departing river steamers. She reached into the glove pocket and removed the parking ticket she had found attached to her windscreen, and crumpled it in a ball and thrust it out of sight. She never got parking tickets, never.

Rain bounced off the road. It was not quite dark, but so much darker that she switched on her sidelights. Coming to the turning where the signpost indicated five miles to the village, she slackened speed again. By the 'Mad Woman's Cottage' (roofless, uninhabited by mad or sane for forty years) a fallow buck leapt across the road, and she stopped to watch it bound over the meadow and disappear in the rainy mist before it reached the woods.

She passed through the village. The light was shining in the Graham Arms. Colin's dented old Citroën was in the car-park, but Fiona was not tempted to join her brother. For all she knew, anyway, he might have left it there days ago, taking a taxi home and feeling no subsequent inclination to retrieve the car. Colin wasn't her problem. He might be everyone's problem, but Fiona had resigned. Colin would drink to that. 'Let Austin have his swynke to him reserved', he would say.

What right had he? 'Everyone suddenly burst out singing'—that was another of his lines—'and I was filled with such delight/As prison birds must find in freedom

8

. . .' She wanted to scream at him, find something of your own to say; but whatever Colin borrowed became his own. His mind was composed now of others' rags and tags.

She pulled the car into a lay-by, a picnic place, which Gavin had first opposed—'I don't want a lot of blighters in Japanese cars eating quiche at my bloody gates'—and then overnight welcomed, having formed the theory that the picnic place would attract visitors to the holiday cottages he had recently converted from an old steading. Experience had not supported the theory, but Gavin had forgotten his old opposition, and Fiona had even—admittedly only once—found him sitting at one of the tables with a group of picnickers. There had—further justification—been a bottle of gin on view rather than quiche, but when she had mentioned the thing to Gavin, he had replied in his most pompous style:

'Just showing the flag, old thing. Duty, don't you see. I was passing by and wished them a civil good-day, and they asked me to have a spot. Couldn't very well refuse. Would have seemed stand-offish. 'Sides, public relations, sometimes think country life's nothing but public relations these days, the way all the good folk from the suburbs spill out into the country. And they don't know a bloody thing, not a bloody thing. So I try to put them right . . .'

She was shaking and in tears. She sobbed while Dvořák sang his discovery of the New World. She couldn't understand it. She was going home. Which she had made, where she had everything, or almost everything. 'Oh, I know how lucky I am'—that was one of her pet phrases, delivered with a smile that almost always disarmed criticism. But the words that sang through the music were those she was always reproving Rosie for employing: 'It's not fair'.

Nanny met her in the hall, anxious. Fiona called her 'Nanny', to dignify her, or try to, but she wasn't really Nanny as older generations would have recognized the breed. Just Karen, recruited from the village to help with the baby, a neat thin girl, the daughter of a bank clerk who would never be promoted even to manage a small country branch. Karen had no more presence or resources than her father, a nice girl, a nice man, but that was all. Fiona looked on her as one of those whom life would always pass by, and felt responsible for her too.

'We've been so worried. I said to Mummy last night, "It's not like Lady Leslie, not like her at all".'

'Oh really! I telephoned, I was detained, I told you that when I telephoned. Surely you can manage for one night.' But that reproof wasn't fair either; Karen had not been hired to manage. 'Are the children all right?'

She was answered by a whoop and scurrying feet and a small boy threw himself against her.

'Mummy, Mummy.'

She held him off the ground, thrusting her face into the tousled red hair. They mustn't see that she had been crying. She had repaired her face, but no one must see.

'I told Rosie you'd be back before supper. I was right, wasn't I, and I told Karen . . .'

'Yes, darling.'

'Have you brought us anything?'

This from Rosie.

But she hadn't. She always did, though she knew it was spoiling them. But she hadn't. She almost lied. The words 'it's coming' formed in her mind.

'So there you are, old thing.'

Gavin emerged, quite steadily, from the business-room where he kept his guns. He pecked her on the cheek, laid, for a moment, his arm round her shoulders. She turned and kissed his cheek, getting a whiff of gin.

'It's all right,' she said. 'It's all right. Goodness, you would think I'd been gone a month.'

'You must have brought something.' Rosie fingered her bag. 'Is it in here?'

'Oh God, for God's sake, stop it. Don't be such a little bitch.'

Rosie's mouth opened wide, ready to wail.

'I say, old girl, steady on. Mummy's tired. She's only ten, Fi, and you do usually bring the kids something. Always said it was a mistake, but you do, you know.'

'I knew you wouldn't this time,' Charlie said. 'I told Rosie so. I was right, wasn't I? I fell off Scamp, Mummy.'

'Did you, darling?

'Yes, at a double oxer. I 'spect I'll have a bloody big bruise, but I didn't cry.'

'Don't say "bloody", darling. Brave of you not to cry.'

'It wasn't a double oxer. He doesn't even know what a double oxer is, Mummy. It was only a pimpsical pole and Scamp didn't even try to jump it. He just refused and Charlie fell over his shoulder. It wasn't anything, Mummy, just a weeny weeny fall.'

'I expect it was very sore all the same.'

'Look here, kids,' Gavin said. 'You just run along, run along, damn you, I said run along. Karen, will you bloody take them upstairs and get them ready for bed . . .'

'Daddy said bloody, why can't I . .?'

'I don't know what you pay that girl for, she has absolutely no control. I was worried, Fi, I thought you might have forgotten. We have guests, remember, for dinner.'

And she had. But how could she have? But then how could she have forgotten the children's presents, and not even have thought of them, not once?

'No need to worry. I had a word with Mrs Hunter and she's got everything under control and A1.'

Oh God, now she would have to make peace with Mrs Hunter too.

'You look as though you could do with a drink first, old thing. Terrible evening.'

'You're very wise to have stopped off here,' Colin said with a wave of the hand.

'Can we have, um, the same again, please, Mr Smith. Large ones, decidedly large ones. My sister Fiona is a model hostess, Perthshire's answer to Elsa Maxwell, I

11

always say. Or do I mean George Weidenfeld? Who can tell? But the drink doesn't exactly flow.' He brought up the last word as though he had rescued it from oblivion. 'Not by a long chalk, whatever the arcane origins of that phrase. I respect her, of course, but . . . a big but . . .'

He took a ten pound note from his pocket, straightened it out, looked at it as if surprised by its appearance, turned it over once or twice.

'Glamis Castle,' he said. 'Why do you suppose the Royal Bank should put a picture of Glamis Castle on their notes? Do you think they pay Strathmore a royalty? Bet they don't. Wonder if they'd like to put Ramornie—my house, you know—on one? What could one charge them? Not a lot? Daresay you're right. Anyway, Mr Smith, here it is, for what it's worth. Note well, if you present this piece of paper to the Royal Bank, they promise to pay you ten pounds on demand. On demand, you must demand.'

Mr Smith took the note, unimpressed. He had heard it all before. Colin's repertory, like his tweed suit, had seen better days.

'So is this a grand dinner? Is this one of my little sister's smart dos? Or merely a duty dinner for assorted bores of the neighbourhood?'

Tony Lubbock had scarcely exchanged a word with his wife. She never enquired about his business now, and he knew she had come to think of it as something disreputable. She read the sort of papers and watched the sort of telly programmes that were always on about shady doings in the City, and greed—'conspicuous greed' they called it, as if 'hidden greed' would be more acceptable —and how the City was failing industry and suchlike crap. Tony could have told them where to put their opinions, and, five years back, would have enjoyed doing so. Now he let it slide. Confined himself to a mental two fingers. Bloody fools. Still, it went against the grain to be supporting such a set of wankers. Susie—called herself Sue now—wasn't slow to spend the stuff. That trouser suit wasn't picked up at a chain store. But that was England—safe haven for pink parasites.

They were on the run though.

She had been waiting for him to get back in order to leave herself. Was it Married Women Against Rape or the Chilcott Green Action Group (formed to drive some poor bugger of a builder into backruptcy, as far as he understood their intentions)? To hell with it, stuff the lot. He took a bottle of Remy Martin from the corner cabinet, and a big balloon glass, and settled in front of the telly.

A woman with metallic hair and a metallic voice was making a point about the Social Services.

'Fuck you,' Tony Lubbock said. 'Only, nobody would.'

He flicked the remote control.

'And you,' Colin said, 'are Enid, and you, Arthur? Have I got that right? The right way round? And you are new to up here, what, if we were further North and West, might be called White Settlers? Important to get these things straight.'

'Not so straight,' the woman, Enid, said. She had been pretty in sharp gamine style, but was now only sharp. She wore her hair in a ragged fringe to suggest the girl she had been. A jewelled cross bounced between her breasts.

'Not so straight,' she said again. 'My grandfather came from these parts. So, when Arthur took early retirement from the company, I said, I don't want Spain or Portugal, thank you very much, it's Scotland for me. So we moved up lock stock and barrel and have never regretted it.'

'Early days yet,' Arthur said, as if the moment for regret might lurk round the next week-end, 'but the natives seem friendly.'

'We do, do we?'

'Don't count chaps like you, of course, not as natives.'

'No, I suppose not, and yet who could be more so?'

'You're here all the time yourself, are you?' Enid said.

13

'Oh quite.'

'Come on, girl, drink up.' Arthur shot his cuffs and examined his watch. 'I make it exactly seven forty-two. It will take us by my reckoning twenty-two minutes from here. So we want to leave in—yes, yerss, three and a half minutes.'

'Arthur was in the RAF before he went into plastics,' Enid said. 'That's where he got this thing about punctuality. I like to be late myself, just a little. He's an Air Commodore you know, but he doesn't use the rank.'

'Fact is, old boy, the days when service rank was an advantage in business are over and done with.'

'Are they now? I suppose you're right. Early retirement—what a beautiful phrase! What depths it suggests! What vistas!'

'The company were against it,' Enid said. 'They wanted Arthur to stay on, but with the takeover, it wouldn't have been the same.'

'No,' Colin said. 'I suppose not. How could it be? But you have each other.'

For a moment they looked baffled or embarrassed. Then Enid gave a crow of laughter.

'I know your type. You make a joke of everything, don't you? I like a laugh myself. All right, Arthur, I'm coming. We'll see you again.'

'I hope so. Devoutly.'

'Might have a game of golf,' Arthur said.

Colin watched them out of the bar, watched Arthur dangle a raincoat over his wife's head as they marched to the BMW, watched them drive off.

He waggled the gin in his glass.

'I think I'm losing my touch, Mr Smith. Well, *eheu fugaces, eheu fugaces.*'

Fiona had steadied herself. She had spoken to Mrs Hunter, praised her dinner arrangements, congratulated Karen on the flowers on the dining-room table, showered, changed, attended to her make-up, dabbed Opium on her temples and wrists, made peace with

Rosie, kissed her good-night, admired Charlie's bruise, kissed him (which he still liked, thank goodness), all in less than forty minutes, and was down in the drawing-room ready for her guests. Gavin's sister, Caro (recently returned from the United States where she had been working for a PR firm some way off Madison Avenue) said to her:

'I've taken two telephone calls for you. A man. Wouldn't give his name. Twice, within a quarter of an hour. Sounded demanding.'

'When was this?'

'Either side of seven o'clock. Car phone, lots of static.'

'I can't think who it could be.'

The ice rattled in her glass. She looked out beyond the lawn and the shrubbery; the hills couldn't be seen. A low sheath of rain cloud cut them off. Fiona adjusted a painting of deer on a summer evening which she had bought the previous summer at the local Art Exhibition in aid of the Cathedral Fund.

'This was a mistake. It's no good. I can't think how I ever thought it was. I must have been mad. Don't you agree? It's absolutely insipid.'

'Amateur work,' Caro said.

'He's an art teacher, I think.'

'It's still amateur work. You can't fool me on paintings, Fi, that's one thing I do know something about.'

'No,' Fiona said. 'It seems I can fool myself.'

'I don't suppose you thought it was really good. You just felt obliged to buy something.'

'Well, yes, but I hung it.'

'Lady of the manor.'

They were almost different generations, for Caro was Gavin's half-sister. She was only twenty-five, a child. But Fiona didn't think of her as so much younger. And Caro, with striking ugly-good looks, a big mouth, a jaw not quite set straight, big brown eyes, dark skin, dark-bay hair cut jagged, had nothing childish in her appearance. She stretched out long legs in black velvet trousers, and smiled at Fiona.

15

'Did he leave a number?'

'The demanding chap? No, said he would call again.'

'Well, I hope he doesn't do so during dinner.'

'You could always unplug the phone.'

'Oh, I couldn't do that.'

'Why not? I always do in my apartment. You do too much for others, Fi. You shouldn't let them run your life.'

III

Fiona gave dinner parties, once or twice a month, in determined conscientious spirit. She had set herself to do so when she married Gavin fourteen years previously. She was not a natural hostess, could for her own part have done very well without them. But as she said, 'If you once let things slip if you live in the country, it's no time at all before you are seeing nobody and eating in the kitchen. I've seen it happen to so many people. Or they take a tray in front of the television. Well, Gavin and I do that sometimes, if there's a good serial, or during Wimbledon. But you've got to keep society going. Otherwise, heaven knows what country life would be like.'

So, once or twice a month, people were assembled. She kept a little book in which she noted down the guests and the menus. She liked to mix up the former, old reliables and family on the one hand; newcomers and visitors on the other. She was shocked when she heard that Liz Lumsden-Fraser was doing dinners commercially for paying guests.

'Well, I'm sorry,' Liz said, 'but I like having people about and I bloody well can't afford to feed them for free. Besides, they love it, Americans especially of course. An agency books them in. I don't mind putting your name up to them if you like, Fi.'

'Thanks, but we haven't come to that yet.'

'Oh it's great fun, you get a change of bores, you see.'

Fiona had fixed on ten as the ideal number. Actually she knew that eight was more satisfactory, but, besides Gavin and herself, there was so often at least one other member of the family there—Caro for instance tonight,

Caro's brother Kenneth, even Colin, or one of their many cousins, with spouse—that she had fixed on ten so that outsiders shouldn't feel too excluded by family chat.

Liz was actually coming tonight too. She was a sort of cousin of Gavin's but didn't count as one for a reason Fiona could no longer remember.

As for the menu, that was always conservative. She had never descended to the vulgarity of *nouvelle cuisine*, even though Mrs Hunter could have managed it competently. Actually, Fiona thought, *nouvelle cuisine* was a natural extension of the sort of elaborate decorative prissiness that magazines had taught the Women's Institute to indulge in, more and more since they had dropped the word 'Rural'. A typical *nouvelle cuisine* plate would be absolutely unremarkable in the displays put on in the so-called Industrial Tent at the local agricultural show. She must remember to share this thought with Caro, who had however gone to the door to admit the first guests.

That shouldn't have been necessary. Fiona and Gavin still employed a butler. That is to say, they had till recently, even if 'butler' like 'nanny' conjured up the wrong image. He had been a sort of general factotum, who looked after the cars and mowed the lawn and drove one of the Land Rovers at the shooting. Apart from waiting at table at the fortnightly dinner parties, his only butlery task had been to clean the silver. But last month Greig had left, explaining that his wife was not happy in the lodge. She wanted him to take a job where they could buy their own house. It was a matter of looking to the future. Since his mother had worked for the family for forty years, this was another blow delivered at the tottering inherited structure. He might be replaced, but the replacement couldn't be thought of as a retainer.

So tonight it was Caro who had answered the door and ushered in Arthur and Enid Kemsley-Smith, punctual to the minute.

They were awkward as first arrivals, would have been

18

awkward as such even if Fiona had been her usual self, since she didn't know them, had only met Enid once briefly since they bought Killinin. But that made them neighbours, and if they were settling, then it was her duty to invite them to dinner. Enid had been quick to tell her that her grandfather had come from these parts, but had been unable to offer further precise information.

Now Arthur talked about the weather and the drive over. Then they discussed the difficulties of upheaval and settling in a new place. Then he talked about the local golf course.

'Bit disappointed. I'd hoped for something a bit better in Scotland. Do you know, I hit a sheep at the fourth yesterday. Well, they won't believe me at Worplesden when I tell them that.'

The telephone rang.

Fiona said, 'Will you take it, Caro? If it's him again, take a message and say I can't speak this evening.'

'Don't you just loathe the telephone?' Enid said. 'If it wasn't that it's the only way the children have communicated since they went to Prep School, I wouldn't bother with it. I'd have it ripped out.'

Fiona didn't believe her.

'How many children have you?' she said.

'Well, they're not children now of course, though I still think of Rupert as a child. He wouldn't like that, he's at Cambridge. I'm much younger than Arthur, you know. And then there are the twins, Mark and Penny. They're twenty-five. Mark's in the City and Penny works in publishing. Well, most girls do, I find. I was able to fix that up for her of course, through my connections.'

Fiona didn't follow this—not that it mattered. She was distracted by Liz's arrival, accompanied by a blond young man in tight white trousers and a flowered shirt.

'Hope you don't mind,' Liz said. 'It's Rory's day for getting drunk. I'd forgotten that when I accepted. So this is Jason, he's some sort of cousin from Oz.'

'Oh really, Liz.'

'Well, all right, he's not a cousin, but he is from Oz.'

'Are you really called Jason?'

'Sure, why not?'

He had rather a nice smile.

'It's just that one can never believe a word Liz says, that's all. But you probably know that already.'

She handed him a drink.

'I hope gin-and-tonic's all right. It's all there seems to be.'

'No,' Caro said. 'She asked me to give you a message. If you leave your name and number, she'll call you in the morning.'

But Tony Lubbock wouldn't. He couldn't sit waiting for a call. Besides he had meetings, he couldn't remember how many, things were moving so fast on so many fronts. But he had this itch. He couldn't account for it.

'No,' he said. 'She really can't speak tonight? I'll call her then.'

'And what about a name?'

He rang off. Clutching his brandy he went through to the kitchen, took a piece of prime fillet from the freezer and stuck it in the microwave. When it was cooked, he waited till it was cool enough to handle and ate it as if it had been a hunk of bread.

Liz said: 'No, you see, my husband gets drunk according to a routine, for medical reasons he says. It does something for the gastric juices. That's his line anyway.'

'We really loved Sydney,' Enid said.

'I'm from Melbourne myself.'

'I've said for twenty years,' Arthur said, 'that if I was twenty years younger, I'd give Australia a chance. It's the country of the future.'

'Used to be,' Liz said. 'Now it stinks. That's right, isn't it, Jason?'

'That's right.'

The dinner was simple. That was Fiona's style. Salmon mousse, followed by gigot of roebuck with new potatoes, runner beans and rowan jelly, then gooseberry tart. It couldn't be faulted. Fiona had decided early in marriage that she couldn't stand a dinner party where she was worried about whether the food would be up to scratch. The wine had been Gavin's province for years. Recently she had taken it over. It was much better now: an Alsatian riesling with the mousse, then some quite decent claret from a shipper in Leith, and a couple of bottles of Château Climens with the dessert.

'Fiona's dos are very tasteful,' Colin would say. Well, she didn't mind, and it was this evening a relief—a very small one—to think that there was nothing that could be criticized.

She didn't eat much herself and struggled to keep abreast of the conversation. Caro was watching her, perhaps anxiously, so she smiled and rallied.

'Jason's a dancer. He's going to put something on at the festival.'

'I might . . .'

The festival was Liz's pigeon. She had started it, bullied the council and local businesses to support it, and extracted a grant from the Scottish Arts Council.

'That took some doing,' she said. 'I had a definite suspicion I was viewed as elitist.'

So now Jason smiled again, showing teeth, and said, 'I might. Liz is twisting my arm hard.'

'He danced with the Australian National Company,' she said.

'The assistant director was gay. That's why I left. He couldn't keep his hands off me. I guess I suffered sexual harassment. But choreography's what I'm really into.'

Dallas Graham, on Fiona's left, shot a glance at Jason, returned his attention to his gooseberry tart. He had been almost silent throughout the meal, something she would normally have noticed and corrected.

'How's the book going?' she said.

'There's only one thing to be said for writing detective novels. Liz will never ask me to do a reading.'

'She might. You're getting well-known, aren't you.'

'Nobody gives readings from detective novels. Too boring for words. Are you all right? You look a bit under the weather.'

'"Well, the weather," she said . . .'

At the far end of the table Gavin had roused himself to reproach Mansie Niven, their MP, for the Government's plan to amalgamate the local regiment, the Breadalbane Highlanders, with their traditional rivals.

'It's a bloody disgrace. You should be more active in the campaign, Mansie. It's not going well.'

'Waste of time,' Mansie said, eyes bloodshot and bow-tie askew, 'the sort of shits we have in the party now, the sort of shits we have as ministers'—his hand crept under the table to feel Caro's thigh—'you might as well . . .'

'Do you mind?' Caro said.

'What? Oh? you might as well try to persuade them to send all the nig-nogs back to nig-nog land.'

Dallas sipped his Perrier.

'I don't know how Mansie does it,' he said to Fiona. 'You'd think somebody would have cut his throat by now.'

'People like your brother-in-law Andrew,' Mansie shouted. 'That's the new breed of Tory. Knows the price of everything and the value of nothing, tight-arsed little climber. And he's climbed into an under-secretaryship after two years in the House.'

'Andrew's rather sweet,' Liz said. 'And he makes me laugh, which is more than you do, Mansie.'

'We met your other brother earlier today,' Enid said. 'What a charmer.'

'Oh Colin. Well Colin is rather different from Andrew . . .'

Tony Lubbock lounged back in a deep armchair. The empty bottle lay on its side on the carpet by his feet. The cigar between his lips had extinguished itself. His eyes were closed. He heard the front door open, heard his wife enter, heard her go upstairs. He pulled himself up, applied a match to the cigar, stared at the dead screen.

His father used to say: 'You have to go forward, my son. You have to recognize that we can never go back.'

But that was just what he wanted to do. Absurd, Freddy wouldn't understand it, Freddy would be embarrassed. But Freddy would stand by him. He always had. Tony had only once seen Freddy lose his temper—in the Members' Bar at Sunningdale of all places, when some balding, strands-of-yellow-hair, git had sneered something about Freddy's 'sheeny partner'—as if that mattered, even if he had been a Jew, as if the bloody club wasn't stiff with them. He'd thought Freddy was going to hit the man, had had to restrain him, physically. The joke was that Freddy would have been equally indignant if Tony had been a Jew.

He didn't even have a photograph of her, had never been one for that sort of thing. Well, he didn't need one, could see her, so clearly, could hear her, that was the thing. He'd never seen her naked, never in less than a bikini. She'd always insisted on a degree of what he supposed was modesty. He'd had girls who liked nothing better than to parade in the nude, and he'd forgotten them, couldn't put a name or a face or a taste to them. She was different.

How did she remember him? He'd really been afraid she hadn't recognized him in that hotel.

It had been easy getting her married name and address from the clerk at the desk: twenty pounds easy.

Flowers.

Fiona and Gavin had always had separate rooms. There had never been any question of anything else, because that was how Gavin's parents had lived, and how his father and stepmother hadn't. Given his hatred of her, hatred founded in fear, it was odd, to his credit, that he tolerated Caro and Kenneth. But that was Gavin, more complicated than anyone but she supposed.

She sat in front of her dressing-table removing make-up. She wore only a bra and knickers. The room was warm, with old-rose patterned curtains open to the night

23

air. The rain had stopped, but the night was close and moths flew around the table-lamp. A dog fox barked from the plantation of larches beyond the pond.

At the age of thirty-seven Fiona Leslie had everything to which she had ever aspired, and was afraid. Fear and self-disgust had run through the length of her affair with Kevin, corrupting further what had started as corrupt. The coarse brutal image of her mother frightened her; that path lay exposed before her, even as Kevin himself had first been encountered as her mother's boy-friend. She slid her hands along her thighs, squeezing the flesh. It was all right; she had escaped, it was over, she had come through. And she had come through more beautiful than she had ever been. Beautiful for the first time in her opinion; she had always compared her looks to those of her sister Belinda, to her own disadvantage, condemning herself as 'merely pretty'. 'Chocolate-box' might have been coined for her. She no longer felt that inferiority. Should she be grateful to Kevin?

No, she felt vulnerable. That was his real legacy, this awareness of vulnerability. She knew how people saw her: cool, self-possessed, stuck-up bitch (Kevin's description that last one, towards the end). But she wasn't like that at all.

She had married Gavin for the house, the estate, the position—only last of all for himself. Which of them had she wronged in doing so? Would Gavin be different if she had been different? Stupid question.

IV

It was a good afternoon after a bad week. Kenneth lay back on cushions while the girl punted them up towards Grantchester. He trailed his hand in the water and watched her. She dug the punt pole in deep and bent her knees. When she straightened them the frayed hem of her denim shorts quivered and her sun-gold legs shone. His eyes were half-closed and she shimmered in the dappled sunlight. Then she sat down and using the paddle eased the punt under a willow. She thrust the pole into the mud to act as an anchor.

'Come on,' she said.

So he crawled forward and took the rope and wound it round the trunk of the tree and tied a loose knot. Then he lay back again and she came to him and he brushed her short dark hair away from her brow and kissed her, first on the eyelids and then on the lips. She put her arms round him and crawled over him.

'I do like this,' she said. 'Do you like it as much as I do?'

He kissed her again and fumbled with her shorts.

'Come on,' she said, 'no one can see us. I don't care anyway.'

She nibbled his lip.

'I could eat you, Kenneth Leslie,' she said.

'The predatory female.'

'Don't talk like that.'

'That was nice,' she said, 'but would you prefer it if I was a boy?'

'No, I don't think so.'

'You don't think so?'

'Mmm.'

'I could be a boy if you like. Kenny, would you like me to be a boy for you?'

'No, stay a girl, Kat. I . . .'

'Sure? It might be fun to be a boy for you.'

'Sure.'

'Oh, all right. You're really not very adventurous, are you . . .?'

He had seen her for six months, known her for two, fancied her from the start. Now they had been lovers for a month and she had buggered up his exams, no question of that. Well, yes, there was a question: she had buggered up his last chance of repairing damage.

'I do love bonking, don't you?' she said.

He also loved her face, her figure and her voice. He loved her voice especially; it was tinny, suburban, assured. He loved that assurance and he loved the fact that there was nothing behind it. She was South London, eighteen, in her first year at King's, reading Law.

'I want to make money,' she said, 'My dad's fifty and doesn't make twenty K. He's a teacher. They're both teachers. Don't get me wrong. I love them, but I don't want that life for myself.'

'What would they think if they saw us now?'

'Dad would be shocked. I guess Mum would be jealous, she reads a lot of junk novels. It's your accent that would shock Dad. He's old-fashioned Labour, CND, Anti-apartheid, and he has no time for the idle rich.'

'I'm not rich.'

'I notice you don't dispute the charge of idleness.'

'Spoken like a prosecuting counsel.'

'I'm not going to be that sort of lawyer. There's no money in crime work. Anyway, I don't intend to practise at the Bar. European Company Law, that's why I'm going to Düsseldorf to work up my German.'

'As my friend Colin would say, "if I was wearing a hat I would take it off to you".'

'Who's Colin?'

'It's too hot to explain. Besides, you mightn't see the point of him.'

'Pretty pointless then.'

In his ground floor rooms in the Great Court of Trinity he opened a bottle of champagne. They drank from the same glass, listening to Charlie Parker.

'I don't see the point of this music either,' she said.

'Oh dear.'

'But I do see the point of champagne.'

'Good. . . . I should get ready.'

She leaned over and kissed him.

"'Nother quick bonk first . . .'

Afterwards, she said: 'This evening sounds weird. You really wear all that gear . . .' she gestured towards the velvet knee-breeches, long coat, ruffled shirt, jabot and buckled shoes.

'It's the Club uniform,' he said, feeling a fool.

'Weird. I want to watch you dress. Is that a wig?'

'I'm afraid so.'

'Christ.'

'Anway I'm going to take a shower first.'

'I'll wait for you.'

He sang in the shower, exhilarated and redeemed. She couldn't know what she had done for him. It didn't matter what else she had done, because she had done this which was so good. When he returned she was wearing a big shaggy sweater of his and nothing else. It almost covered her buttocks.

He was proud of the Club, which was said to be the oldest dining-club in the University, so he pretended it was all a joke.

'Who else is in it?'

He named some of the members, choosing those of whom she might have heard without disapproval.

'Christ, if Dad was here, he would say you were in "the Wrong Set" my boy. Set of creeps.'

'They're all right.'

'And you're Nelson Mandela. Who's this guest you have coming?'

'He's called Andrew Meldrum.' He straightened the

27

grey wig which had seen better days. 'He's a Tory MP,
I'm afraid.'

'Another creep. I've seen him on the telly. How come
he's your guest?'

'Well, his sister's married to my brother, and when he
asked to come, I couldn't very well say no. I don't like
him much, to tell the truth.'

'And he gets his kicks dressing up in funny costumes
to get plastered with boys like you. Jee-sus, what a story
for the tabloids.'

'Resist the temptation.'

'I might.'

'I love you.'

'Oh love. Don't like that word.'

And it might be true; she might not be ready. But he
was. She had her career marked out, programmed; she
knew where she was going. He watched her cross the
court till she disappeared through the Gate, and the
porter's head turned to follow her progress into Trinity
Street.

Kenneth knew of course that the 'Brothers Club' was
absurd; membership was nonetheless gratifying. It
might not be the oldest dining-club in the University; the
distinction was disputed by the 'True Blue'; but it was
certainly old. The minute books went back to 1744 and its
first patron was Henry St John, Viscount Bolingbroke. It
took its name from the club Bolingbroke himself had
founded in 1711 in rivalry of the Whig Kit-Kat. Tories
(mostly Jacobites) had been rare in eighteenth century
Cambridge, when the University still maintained its
Puritan, Roundhead, Whig character; all the more exclu-
sive for their rarity of course. It had long lost any political
connection or interest, though in the nature of things
most members probably would vote Conservative, if
they voted at all.

'In my day,' Colin had said, when Kenneth mentioned
his election, 'it was exclusively queer, very queer. I dined
as a guest once, and had my virtue assailed by a plump

young man who now plays character parts on the telly. I saw him as a vicar in an inept comedy the other day. Sic transit gloria Randy, I said to myself.'

It wasn't like that now; not exactly. All the same he wondered whether it was the memory of Colin's reminiscences that had prompted his brother Andrew to angle for an invitation. Andrew had always been discreet, though he had once made a pass at Kenneth. The summer of Belinda that was. Strange to think how he had adored her that year of Grace's death, and now . . . he didn't even know where she was. He took another glass of champagne, placing his lips over the smudge made by Kat's mouth.

Andrew arrived only a quarter of an hour late. He had gone straight from the station to his hotel to change, and then had had to wait for a taxi. He was wearing a smoking-suit in the green-and-blue Breadalbane tartan and a floppy green bow-tie. The suit was made of a wool-and-silk mixture.

'I hesitated before buying it,' he said, 'I was afraid it might make me look like Mansie Niven. Of course I've never dared to wear it in my constituency, but I thought to-night, as a treat . . .'

'Have some champagne,' Kenneth said, 'we're not expected for another ten minutes or so.'

Few, if any, were sober, by the time the seventh (and last) course, angels on horseback, was set before them. The man on Kenneth's left, Colm McStay, the guest of the Club President whose uncle he was, prodded at them with a fork.

'I'm suspicious of they wee beasts in June,' he said. He was a well-known political journalist, who had retained traces of his Glasgow accent, as a result of which he was much in demand from TV producers. Kenneth had heard his politics described as 'well to the Right of Genghis Khan, makes Maggie look like an inside-left'. He had himself read an article in which McStay, though a Roman Catholic, had argued that the solution to the

Ulster problem could only be the re-incorporation of the Republic of Ireland in the United Kingdom. 'I'm a Catholic Unionist,' he was fond of saying. 'What's wrong with that?'

During the meal however he had talked principally of boxing.

'The greatest pound-for-pound fighter of them all was Sugar Ray Robinson. He would have licked any of the boys around now with his left hand alone. Wonderful: I saw his fight with Joey Maxim in Madison Square Garden when I was a boy and staying with my mother's brother who was Bishop of Baltimore. The heat beat Robinson that night; it was a hundred and ten in the Garden, and he couldn't get off his stool for the fourteenth when he was the length of Third Avenue ahead on points. Greatest exhibition I've ever seen. And now I'm told he's dying in poverty. Sad, but that's boxing for you. Magnificent as war, and indefensible as war. Are you a fan yourself?'

Now he pushed the angels on horseback aside, and asked the waiter to bring him another helping of Crème Brûlée.

'They don't make it anywhere like Trinity.'

'No, it's the speciality of the kitchen.'

'Aye, I've always had a sweet tooth. I get it from my sainted mother who liked nothing better than a good afternoon tea at the St Enoch Hotel. You're from Scotland yourself, you say. You'll no bide in that sad country, will you?'

'Why do you call it sad?'

'Because it's a place to leave. Sad, defeated, self-pitying. Mind you, I'm not saying we shouldn't send the likes of Andrew Meldrum back there. What did you want to bring a wanker like that to spoil an evening like this for?' He leaned across Kenneth. 'I'm calling you a wanker, Andrew.'

'Oh, I manage a bit more than that sometimes.'

It was a tradition of the Club that they drank claret after

the meal, rather than port, the latter being condemned as a Whig beverage. It was also a tradition that guests and new members should be invited (required in the case of new members) to down a bumper in one. It was served in a silver tankard that held an imperial pint. Colm McStay declined.

'I've been a guest here before, so I count myself excused.'

Instead, his nephew had arranged to have him supplied with a bottle of Talisker.

Andrew however complièd, and lowered the empty tankard amidst cheers. Then he slipped away to vomit.

'Prudent,' Colm McStay said. 'But he's letting down his guard. You're no' his boy-friend, are you?'

'No, not at all.'

He explained the connection.

'I'm glad to hear it. I was wondering what a nice boy like you was doing with Andrew Meldrum. Of course, he's riding high now. Herself thinks the sun shines out of his arse. He used to help write her speeches you know, and lick her arse, if I'm not getting too many arses muddled in this sentence. But his guard's slipping. It always happens. Chaps like Andrew are careful till success goes to their head and they think they can get away with anything. I've seen it often enough. And the terrible thing is, it's just a wee bit of success that's enough to destroy their equilibrium.'

Later the party broke up, its members finding their way to different sets where other people appeared, more bottles were produced, and new parties were formed, as the evening turned into a species of country-dance. Girls were not absent, laughing at the members of the Brothers Club in their ridiculous, if in some cases fetching, costumes. All the undergraduates had finished their exams; they would soon be dispersing. In high summer, Kenneth caught a whiff of autumn. He lay back in a deep chair, smoking a cigar which he was not sure he wanted, but which he was disinclined to extinguish.

Someone had put an old Stones record on the gramophone: rebellion turned to nostalgia. Colin claimed to have been in Paris in May '68: 'even at the time I saw it was absurd. Of course I was ten years too old.' Kenneth on the other hand felt the sweet attraction of that decade in which he had been born: its promise that the world would be created anew, without hypocrisy. The promise itself had been false; but it must have been nice to have such hope.

He had wasted years behind him, years without a serious impulse. He had played with people, whom for convenience he called friends, who pretended that the modern world was irrelevant; Kenneth had spent autumn days shooting pheasants in Suffolk, till, at the beginning of this academic and sporting year, their host had brusquely declared that all the shooting had been taken by a syndicate of City men, and that he had retained none for his son and his son's friends: 'the birds have to pay for themselves now. It's a commercial enterprise running an estate . . .'

Kat was the one true thing he had encountered. Kat tore the curtain of make-believe away. She exposed the sham of the two cults according to which Cambridge lived: the cult of the gentleman (itself unpopular now, ridiculous in the eyes of most dons, and resented by them) and the cult of scholarship itself. She admired only those dons who commuted between Cambridge and London, where they provided legal or financial advice, or alternatively moved with undisguised greed along the corridors of influence, selling their opinions to the highest bidder. Kat knew what she wanted, knew she was going to get it. At present Kenneth was included in her list of desires. For how long? He couldn't keep pace with a girl so well attuned to the world. It was true she made him feel more truly himself; but what good was that when that self was so indeterminate, so much more ready to see a joke than an opportunity?

'Who,' Andrew Meldrum laid his hand on Kenneth's

shoulder and, kneeling, whispered in his ear, 'who is that piece who has just come in?'

He pointed to a long-legged boy with soft blond hair, pale skin and rather thick Jaggerish lips. He wore jeans and a T-shirt with a message in Cyrillic script. He dangled an open bottle of champagne.

'No idea.'

'Whoever he is, I must have him.'

He hurried across the room before anyone else could seize the newcomer and slipped his arm round his waist. The boy turned towards him and let himself be kissed. They subsided on to the floor, the sofa being already occupied by their host—an Indian post-graduate who had played Orsino in the college production of *Twelfth Night*, and the girl who had played Viola; or perhaps it was her brother, Kenneth couldn't be sure; they were indeed twins, children of a famous theatrical family, and Rashid, their host, would have been indifferent as to which he made love to.

Kenneth drank some more whisky and re-lit his cigar. The boy whom Andrew was embracing detached himself sufficiently to take a swig from his champagne bottle; then he thrust it into Andrew's mouth.

V

Fiona woke with a headache. It was six o'clock. She
sipped Malvern Water, reluctant to take an aspirin.
Disturbed by her movement, Mushtaq, the smokey-blue
Persian, leapt off the pillow and stalked in resentment
towards the window. He sat down, thrust his left hind
leg high in the air, and licked his bottom. Solomon, the
Labrador, shifted at her feet, sighed deeply, and
returned to sleep. She could hear Gavin snore through
the bedroom wall.

Gavin represented 'all this', which Fiona cherished.
He was the cause of 'all this'. Without him she wouldn't
have it. The hills across the valley were still hidden in
mist, but the mist was thinning even as she watched; it
was going to be hot. Without Gavin she wouldn't have a
bedroom from which she could watch the mist clearing
from the hills. She thought of friends who lived in
Edinburgh and London, and of how their lives were
circumscribed by stone, bricks, mortar, the pressing
awareness of other people breathing in their thousands,
however early you woke. However early, you couldn't
escape that awareness.

Seeing her settled, Mushtaq light-footed back, and
rubbed his shoulder against her face. She buried her
nose in the soft fur, loving the cat for its affection
founded on selfishness. That was the trouble with
Gavin: he was so apologetic, so eager to please her. He
had never reproached her even during the first months
of her infatuation with Kevin, before the affair turned
leaden with disappointment, sour with reality lingering
like a habit of which she was ashamed, but which she
could not bring herself to break: something dirty,

degrading, yet part of her, answering some need. It was Gavin's bloody humility, the way he didn't answer back, allowed her to ride over him: all that infuriated her and made her want to hurt him.

She envied Liz who rubbed along with Rory on such an easy basis, in a friendship that allowed them blazing rows; neither made any demand on the other beyond what was acceptable. Gavin made such demands. He wanted her approval, even admiration, which she couldn't give. He wanted her to admire his loyalty, his mute suffering.

'Is there anything wrong?' he would say. 'You're very silent.'

'What's the point of saying anything when we never say anything that matters?'

When Fiona was young she had once overheard her sister Belinda say,

'I don't know what Fiona cares about, except clothes and her appearance.'

'She's quite keen on hockey,' someone—who? She couldn't remember—had replied.

She stretched her legs, producing a rumble of protest from Solomon. She ought to get up. She wanted to get up. Rising early, while the other members of the household slept, was one of her chief pleasures. Asked to give an account of her ideal day, she would have said it began with early rising, a walk round the loch with the dogs, in a silence broken only by natural sounds, or perhaps a ride through the birch woods and up onto the moor.

But today, Liz had reminded her last night, there was a meeting of the Festival Committee at half-past ten. The boy Jason was clearly Liz's latest. Well, good luck to her. He was rather dishy. He was the sort of young man Belinda would have . . . the way she had with Kenneth. . .

Fiona gave the world an impression of self-confidence. She knew that, and was proud of it. She had worked hard to make that impression, to hide her fears that

Belinda was right: that she was shallow, what they used to call a clothes-horse.

It was absurd to worry about her sister's judgement at her age. It wasn't anyway as if Belinda had made anything of her own life.

Two hours later, she had bathed, dressed, taken Solomon and the spaniels for a walk to the stables and back, and breakfasted with Rosie and Charlie, half-listening to their chatter as parents do, intervening only to bring a squabble to an end. Gavin passed through the breakfast-room, pecked her on the cheek—did she flinch?—and took a roll and cup of tea through to his business-room, muttering that he was late and had to be in Perth within the half-hour. In a little they saw the Land-Rover disappear round the bend of the drive. The children vanished on ploys of their own. Caro appeared in a dressing-gown, poured herself a cup of coffee and lit a cigarette.

'Those Kemsley-Smiths were the pits.'

'Dire, but . . .'

'But?'

'Neighbours, you know . . .'

Caro laughed. 'Come off it, Fi, you've no need, not with me.'

'It's a part I'm good at. It's the only part I'm good at. What did you think of Jason?'

'Trouble for Liz there.'

'Oh, do you think so? I thought he was rather dishy.'

'Come off it again. I know the type, and so do you. A little shit. Has your boy-friend phoned?'

'Boy-friend? No. I don't know who it could be, so you can't call him that.'

Tony Lubbock half-listened to Radio 4 as he drank his coffee. He made a lot of noise in the kitchen in the morning and often swore at the voices on the radio, hating their tone of concern, which couldn't quite mask their determination never to be caught out in an attitude that wasn't approved by the right people. He felt braced for the new day, like a catapult charged to shoot its missile. He never had hangovers: one thing he had to thank his Ukrainian blood for, as he often said, too often for Susie. He collected his briefcase from the drawing-room, where it rested beside the armchair in which he had gone to sleep before rousing himself to make his heavy-footed way upstairs. The room stank of his cigars, and the brandy bottle lay empty on its side on the Shiraz rug. To hell with it: Francesca, their daily, would be in long before Susie was up. Which was a pity. A horn sounded without; Shane, his driver, was ready to take him to town.

Shane was one of the many things Susie held against him. She disliked any ostentation that brought no benefit to her. She disliked Shane himself anyway. Shane was a good-looking boy from Essex, the child of transplanted East Enders. He was racist, sexist, and full of joyous life. That infuriated Susie, who had learned to believe that such unforgivable social attitudes must spring from resentment, insecurity, and bitterness. Shane was free of all that. He had even had a black girl-friend once; that didn't stop him from cheerful announcements of appalling race prejudice. Susie couldn't understand him. He suited Tony just dandy. He had never been late in the six months he had worked as his driver. He spoke only when Tony wanted conver-sation, and he said nothing that annoyed his boss, and a lot that he agreed with.

He didn't get out of the car to open the door for Tony. That wasn't the way they played it.

'Wotcher, cock.'

'Wotcher, cock.'

They smiled at each other, the parody complete. Then Shane turned round, restored his dark glasses, and slipped the Mercedes into gear.

'Dow Jones is down,' he said, over his shoulder. 'Seems like New York's wet its effing pants.'

Tony grunted, took some papers from his briefcase

and worked for the half-hour they were on the motorway. Then, as they entered the built-up area where the increase of traffic made progress irregular, he turned to the telephone. He spoke to Freddy first, reassured himself that there was nothing of immediate concern likely to hit them on arrival at the office, then rang Fiona's number. He didn't care if Shane listened. He trusted Shane.

'Oh, it's you again,' he said, when Caro answered. 'Do you live by the telephone? Who are you anyway?'

'Who are you, that's more to the point—?'

'Look, just put Fiona on, will you?'

'Well, who shall I say's calling? She might not want to speak to you?'

But he didn't want to give her warning, not because he feared that she would decline to come to the telephone, not that at all, but rather because he wanted to hear how she responded to his 'it's me, Tony . . . you didn't think I was going to let you slip away again, did you?'

And so he waited in silence till Caro said,

'Oh very well then,' and went to fetch Fiona while Tony felt his heart beat faster, and the years fall away from him. He heard her voice, clear and remote as a bell sounding across a valley, and, with a surge, he made his announcement.

'I don't know what you mean, "slip away".'

'You don't?'

'No, it wasn't like that.'

'Worst mistake of my life. Only mistake of my life. Only big one.'

He was lying, of course. It wouldn't have worked then. He hurried on lest she should detect the insincerity. For it could work now. He had known that since the moment he saw her on the steps of the hotel.

'I'm in Scotland again this week-end. I'd like to come and see you . . .'

There was a pause. He imagined her frowning, biting her lower lip. He wondered who was in earshot at her end of the telephone.

'Old friend,' he said, 'picking up the threads, nothing more than that.'

'All right then, come to lunch Sunday.'

'Lunch Sunday. That leaves me a dead Saturday. I finish my business Friday afternoon.'

He was Napoleonic; never reinforce failure, reinforce success: that was how he had worked for twenty years. It had taken him and Freddy from their one-room office off Baker Street to their present glory.

'I've got to take the kids to a Pony Club do on Saturday. You'd be bored.'

'Never bored. I like ponies anyway. I've got a couple of steeplechasers of my own, you know.'

'I didn't.' She laughed. He could feel her mood lighten. 'All right then, come Saturday, stay the night. We've got other people coming. The more the merrier. Bye . . .'

She replaced the receiver without waiting for acceptance or giving him directions, as if she was saying to herself: 'if you really want me, you can bloody well find me'.

He settled back and lit a cigar.

'You don't like my wife much, Shane, do you?'

'Not a lot, Tony.'

'Not a lot. No.'

Gavin was one of those who push brown envelopes to the back of their desk and dread accountants as children do dentists. When he left the firm of solicitors that handled the estate business, he felt as if he had been through a wringer. Young Maconochie (actually a man of thirty-five) who had become senior partner when his father had finally dribbled, with a good deal of persuasion, into retirement the previous year, had spoken to Gavin with a firmness and acerbity that barely disguised contempt. Maconochie was a thruster himself, said to have his hand in a variety of enterprises; his name was mentioned whenever any local development was mooted. It was his mission to wake things up; 'we've been a backwater too long,' he had been heard to say. 'Modernization is Scotland's answer to Socialism,' he had told the Chamber of Commerce in a Presidential address. He had computerized the firm; that had been the last straw for old Maconochie, a decent stick, whose principal ambition had been to be regarded as an equal by the County. To be invited to shoot by Lord Glenbuterol as a friend rather than His Lordship's man of business had been his proudest achievement. Now, bereft of business, he was seeing out his life in the ugly inter-war house he had bought at Blairgowrie, within a long wooden club's distance of the Rosemount Golf Course. His son, who had fretted at the old man's snobbish indolence, now took pleasure in giving a tough time to those clients whom he particularly associated with his father's foolishness. Gavin came near the head of that category.

This morning's meeting had been rougher than most, as he confronted Gavin with the reality of his financial position. The load of accumulated debt grew heavier every year, as mismanagement and ill-conceived schemes of capital expenditure, undertaken by Gavin in moments of foolish optimism, which old Maconochie had not had the sense to oppose, had built up the estate overdraft to a level which it was proving impossible even to service. There was only one way out, Stuart Maconochie insisted. Gavin had just had a stroke of luck. The tenant of one of the outlying farms, near the city boundaries, had recently died, leaving no heir who might be entitled to take over the tenancy. The farm must be sold.

'Of course that will reduce your income by the level of the rent, but that farm needs a lot spent on it—there's been no investment there for twenty years or more—and you can't afford that. This way, you can reduce your indebtedness and give yourself breathing-space to put the remainder of the estate in better order. If you don't act now, you're going to find yourself in very serious trouble whenever the economic climate changes and banks start calling in dodgy loans. And don't fool yourself into supposing that the present conditions of easy credit can last for ever. People make that mistake too easily. A dozen years ago everyone was acting on the assumption that the price of land would go on rising. "They can't make any more of it"—how often I heard my father intone that platitude. The truth is things can't go on as they are, Sir Gavin . . .'

The advice itself was unwelcome, the tone in which it was delivered even more so. If Gavin had been more imaginative, he might have reflected that a clerical ancestor of Maconochie's would have invoked the wrath of the Lord on the sinners of his parish with the same degree of satisfaction. Maconochie had had a good morning; not so Gavin.

'I've a good mind to remove my business from him,' he said, twenty minutes later and already outside a large pink gin, at the bar of the City & County Club.

'Where would you take it? Maconochie's a little shit, but they're all the same, lawyers, shits.'

The speaker was a slight elderly man, Colonel Greenheart, who neither looked nor sounded like a colonel, having a high piping voice and delicate features. He now kept an antique shop and collected erotica.

'Steady on,' said another man at the bar, 'I'm a lawyer myself.'

'Then you ought to be ashamed of yourself. Shits.'

'Spot more gin,' Gavin said. 'Spot more large gin. And for the Colonel. What about you, MacGillvray,' he said to the lawyer.

'I've had my ration, thanks.'

'Ration,' the Colonel squeaked. 'Bloody *ration* of gin. Bought a rather interesting, rather a curious, piece, Gavin, the other day. Like you to see it, value your opinion. Established its provenance. Seems to have been commissioned by old Straloch. I mean the grandfather of the present boy, of course. The old Marquess was . . .' he paused . . . 'a bit of a rip in his day. It's a young girl and a white monkey, and what they're up to I can't quite

41

determine. But interesting, no doubt of that. Touch of the surrealism, I fancy.'

'Oh yes,' Gavin said. 'Bloody rude he was, that's what he was, that's what sticks in my gullet. Love to see your painting, Gerry, not in my line of course, more Fiona's actually.'

'Couldn't show this to Fiona, old boy. Glad that fellow MacGillvray's taken himself off. Just confirms what I've always said. Great mistake to have amalgamated the two clubs . . . that's so, Angus?'

'Couldn't be helped, Colonel,' the steward replied. 'Neither was what they call financially viable on its own. Still, I agree it's not what I would call a comfortable marriage, sir.'

'Contradiction in terms.' Colin, entering the room, caught the tail-end of the observation. 'Can any marriage be described as comfortable? Don't know about yours, Angus, but there was little comfort in mine. Morning Gavin, Gerry. You know Arthur? Course you do, Gavin. He dined at your table last night, *nicht wahr*? Arthur, Colonel Greenheart, Gerry, a man to beware of. Don't be deceived by that pink and white complexion, an evil man. Gerry, Air Commodore—that's the right rank?—Arthur Kemsley-Smith . . . Well, Arthur, here we are. The hub of the county. The clearing-house of gossip. You'd better become a member. Angus, bring the book, will you, please.'

'Don't usually use the rank,' Arthur said. 'Not in Civvy Street. Very cosy little place you have here. Found Colin stranded, and he was kind enough to bring me . . .'

Colin, in Prince of Wales checks, extended an arm. He was at that point of the day when things once again seemed possible.

'Yes, Arthur, you must take out membership. Gerry, will you second him? Splendid. Gavin, you look under the weather. Unburden yourself of your sorrows.'

'Been having a rough morning with young Maconochie . . .'

'Maconochie, Maconochie, there's no one like Maconochie, as Mr Eliot observed. You haven't yet encountered Maconochie, Arthur. He's called the Hidden Flaw. . .'

And so they slipped into afternoon, with gin and toasted cheese sandwiches, and the afternoon began to slide away, with gossip, ribaldry and the bitter-sweet sensation of time being wasted and therefore conquered. The Sea of Faith was on the ebb, as Colin unfailingly remarked; 'which suits me just dandy. To live in an age of faith must be very strenuous.'

'You were in remarkably good form,' Liz said to Fiona.
'Was I?'
'Quite different to last night. I wondered about you last night, didn't I, Jason?'

Jason flicked a strand of hair back, abstracted his gaze from the mirror.

'Too right.'

He swivelled to give Fiona full attention, and flashed a smile disclosing teeth of a perfection rare in Perthshire.

'Liz raved about you, how you were the tops for beauty in the neighbourhood. I guess I was disappointed. I said as much on our drive home, but this morning, wow, I see what she was getting at.'

'Sweet of you.'

'You look as if you'd come into a fortune,' Liz said.

'No such luck. Quite the reverse. Poor Gavin's had a meeting with Stuart Maconochie this morning, being lectured at, I imagine, and told we're just half a step from the Bankruptcy Court.'

'Young Maconochie,' Liz said. 'You don't want to listen to him.'

'No of course not.'

'I don't get it,' Jason said. 'That house you have. Liz was saying Gavin's family had had it for ever. I thought you were rich.'

'Oh rich,' Fiona said. 'Nobody's rich. Not people like

43

us. Not any more. Now what about some lunch. I know, let's be silly and have champagne.'

'Fiona, this isn't like you.'

'I know. That's what's nice. Call it an anti-Maconochie.'

'I don't get it. . .'

'There's a problem,' Wilkins, the general manager of Lubbock-Paynter Investments, said, 'with that Aylesbury development . . .'

'Not another,' Freddy sighed.

"Fraid so. Department of Resource & Development are objecting.'

'Department of Restraint of Development,' Tony said. He knocked the ash off his Upmann Corona. 'So how do we screw them? Who do we screw?'

Over coffee, Jason having gone to the loo, Liz said,

'Thank you.'

'For what?'

'Sounds silly. For what you said about being one step from bankruptcy. I know you were joking, but he doesn't. He doesn't know much, tell the truth, maybe that's why I'm crazy about him. I've always gone for dumb blonds. Rory was blond once, remember.'

'Well, blondish.'

'Now he's dumb and grey, poor lamb. But I could see Jason looking at you . . .'

'When he could take his eyes off the mirror.'

'He is vain, isn't he? Well, he's got a lot to be vain about. Then you said that, and he stopped looking. He's a regular little gold-digger.'

'Oh Liz, be careful.'

'I'm too old to be careful.'

It was only in the last year that they had become such close friends. Previously Fiona had distrusted Liz, disapproved of her once. Perhaps she also was growing too old for care.

'Those Kemsley-Smiths,' Liz said. 'Not quite the thing.'

'Not at all.'

'That Enid, that voice. . .'

'But nice, you know.'

'Oh nice enough, I daresay.'

'And neighbours.'

Arthur was telling a long story about service life, or perhaps about his days in plastics. It was difficult to be sure, for his narrative line wandered. He put his face very close to Colonel Greenheart as he spoke, and then opened his mouth wide and laughed. His shoulders heaved as he did so. This prevented the laughter from being infectious. Gloom settled over the others. Without being requested, Angus made more toasted-cheese sandwiches. He brewed a pot of coffee and sipped cold tea himself, pretending it was the whisky Arthur had just forced on him.

Colin detached himself, returned in a little with his white bull-terrier Sikes.

'Dogs not allowed in the Club, Mr Meldrum.'

'That's all right. Only Sikes. He's trained to keep the lawyers out.'

'And so the popsy stood up in the Mess,' Arthur continued, 'mother-naked, and said, "I've never been so affronted in my life". The Air Vice-Marshal didn't know where to look. He was never the same man after.'

'I suppose not,' Colonel Greenheart said. 'Of course old Straloch—I mean the young man's grandfather—would have been lucky to keep out of jail these days. Under-age servant-girls, that was his line. The old Marchioness had a terrible time with him. Still, it did a lot to counter rural depopulation. He scattered his image far and wide. Angus here has a look of him, don't you, Angus.'

'So they say, Colonel, so they say. Sandwiches anyone?'

'Yes, rank protected him. He had curious tastes too. These days he'd have gone to jail.'

'Jail eh, I don't know about jail,' Arthur said.

'No, why should you? You'd have to ask our friend Dallas Graham about jail.'

45

'Chap who was at dinner last night. He been in jail?'

'Oh, lots of times. Time and again. D & D, cheque fraud, murder, you name it.'

'Murder?'

'Sort of murder.'

'Better go home,' Gavin said. 'Save the estate. Young shit Maconochie.'

'Better not drive, sir. Call you a taxi.'

'You're a four-wheeler,' Colin said. 'Know that story, Arthur? Chap came up to Gilbert—W.S. Gilbert of course—in the club and asked him to call him a cab. "You're a four-wheeler." "What do you mean, sir?" "Well, you asked me to call you a cab and I can't very well call you hansom." Old.'

'Very old.'

'Very old, Gerry, you're absolutely right, but age cannot wither etc. . . .'

The bull-terrier nosed around the room, bumping into tables and chairs.

'I adore them,' Colin said. 'They have no clue.'

'Not fit to drive?'

'No, sir.'

'Always fit to drive'.

'No, sir. Call you a taxi, Sir Gavin.'

'One up to Maconochie if you're done for drunk driving,' the Colonel said. 'Young shit, you know.'

'Got a point there. Call me a taxi, Angus.'

'I adore them. They have no clue.'

'Might charge it to Maconochie.'

'Existentialism and bull-terriers, that's my creed. Ever tell you about my encounter with Sartre, Gerry?'

'Yes, Colin, more than once.'

'Very strange. There I was in the Dôme, or was it the Deux Magots, explaining the whole biznai to this whisky-drinking frog dwarf in a regulation beret, and making rather a good shot at it, considering the number of Pernods I'd had. Had the impression he was getting a grasp of the argument when the waiter approached him and said *'Téléphone, Monsieur Sartre . . .'*

46

'Don't follow,' Arthur said.

'Never mind.'

'Existentialism and bull-terriers.'

A little later they got Gavin into his taxi. It was hot in the street. Colin leant against the wall as Sikes peed on a Mercedes with German plates.

'Good dog. I adore them . . .'

'Yes, Colin, they have no clue. Come and see my painting, both of you. I'd like your opinion. Used to belong to old Straloch, you know—the grandfather of the present boy. Don't know what the monkey's doing to the girl. Value your opinion. Surrealist, you know, more interesting, Colin, than your bloody Existentialism . . .'

'If you wish. Must point out however, bull-terriers are not surrealists. Or only very rarely. . . .'

Fiona took one glance at Gavin, quite enough.

'You'd better go to bed, old thing. Sleep it off.'

'Maconochie. Frightful young shit. Gerry thinks so too.'

'Oh Gerry. That explains your condition.'

'Good friend, Gerry. Best of friends. Arthur there too. And Colin. All good friends.'

He tried to kiss her.

'Go to bed, Gavin, Before the children see you.'

'Children. Nothing to leave them, not if young shit has his way.'

She watched him stumble upstairs, feeling his way like an animal in unfamiliar territory. What was it Colin said about drunkenness? That it made the world and experience always new; something like that, which was a joke really on Colin, since his conversation in liquor was stale, repetitive and far too often heard. Yet, in her strange new mood, in which old certainties seemed to dissolve like the fade out in a black-and-white movie, she had a glimmering of what he meant. She had spent so many years herself, just going through the motions, living on autopilot, experiencing nothing really.

'Fiona's so bland . . .'

Who had said that?

Their ghastly mother, Diana. Well, at least she had done for Diana when she took Kevin off her. The old bitch had crumpled, ageing ten years in a matter of weeks. This victory, which caused her no compunction when she remembered the pain Diana had inflicted on her, was now, for Fiona, the chief justification of that otherwise shaming and ultimately humiliating affair.

And yet hadn't it perhaps been Kevin who, in a sense, had woken her up? He hadn't in the whole course of their relationship said a single thing with which she instinctively agreed. So she had learned something: that other people could live comfortably—and successfully—for there could be no doubt that Kevin was a success—his photographs of famine in Somaliland had been spread right over last week's *Sunday Times*—could then live comfortably and successfully while accepting none of her standards. And yes, that had been an eye-opener, she thought, as she heard Gavin lurch into his bedroom and the door slam. She stood listening till she heard only silence from his room.

As a child she had been afraid of silence. That was something Belinda and Colin (and Andrew, but he never counted for her) had never been ready to concede her: that she was sensitive to atmosphere and had been frightened by silence. And because they didn't concede it, because they were jealous of her when she was a little girl and still her mother's favourite, before Diana all at once started to hate her, the very moment her breasts first showed, they had between them driven her towards that manner and those attitudes they scorned.

It was their refusal to see her as she was, and that sudden revelation that her mother's love had turned to hate (and had that been a premonition of the Kevin saga?), which together had turned her into the model School Monitor; made her, yes, she admitted it, 'the stuck-up little bitch'.

But that was changing, surely. She ran her finger over

the velvet flesh of a peach, dappled by the sun slanting through the open door onto the rich mahogany side-board that held the fruit-bowl. She was no longer that person. She didn't dare to be that person any more.

She had made correctness her god. There was another reason for the worship she had accorded that idol.

In the drawing-room she took down the painting of deer on a summer evening: pretty, wishy-washy, care-ful, dead. Her whole life had been formed by a failure of courage. She had been frightened by Tony; she could admit that now, frightened of the demands he would make, of the world he would expose her to, frightened that she wouldn't live up to what he wanted of her and that he would throw her aside. So she had turned back: to paintings of deer on a summer evening by a river which bore no resemblance to the turbulence of reality.

'What has your husband been doing to my poor Arthur?'

'I should apologize. Gavin was in a bit of a state, I think . . .'

(But why should I apologize; I'm not his keeper. If he and Arthur get fou as puggies, as old Margot Rutherford would put it, what's it to me? It's their business.)

But Enid, it seemed, was not ringing to reproach her.

'Not to worry. Only I haven't seen Arthur like that since the day he broke eighty at Royal Mid-Surrey.'

She gave a crow of laughter; clearly his condition betokened his acceptance by the County.

Girls together, she invited Fiona to agree, superior and forgiving; what jolly dogs their menfolk were.

'It's too terrible. Arthur hasn't the liver for it. Between you and I and the doorpost, I hold my liquor better. And Colin was there too, I gather. I must say, he's quite a chap your brother. And he's got a bull-terrier, Arthur says.'

'Oh yes, he's got a bull-terrier.'

'My favourite dogs, so sweet . . .'

She went on for a long time. Arthur's escapade marked the beginning of a beautiful friendship.

'Anything I can do to help with the festival, I'm only too willing. I don't like to push myself forward, but you will tell Liz, won't you? I'm an experienced adminstrator, you know. And I do like to make myself useful. If you can't be useful in this life, I always say, what good are you? We've all got to make our contribution, don't you agree? You may be as rich as all hell, but if you don't contribute, what good are you? That's what I say, don't you agree?

'Oh yes . . .'

Oh yes, yes, in a manner of speaking. . . .

'Tony, look as if you've had a hard day.'

Ted Brabbington, his father-in-law, never had a hard day, unless you counted eighteen holes of golf hard. Nevertheless, Tony Lubbock wasn't displeased to find that his wife's parents were dining with them. Ted was all right, more than could be said for Debbie, who was in fact Susie's stepmother. It was easy to forget that: Susie called her 'mummy'. Ted, at ease in his son-in-law's house, poured Tony a stiffish J & B, and squirted soda.

'Hard day? Your roses are looking splendid. Been having trouble with greenfly myself . . .'

He gestured at the careful Surrey garden, with its wide-spreading Victorian copper beech, the conifers and laburnums at the fringes of the rolling lawn, the rose-beds smart as the Guards Division on parade, the octagonal summer-house where deck-chairs and other garden furniture were now stored.

'Take a turn,' he said, 'while the girls fix supper.'

'Worried about Susie,' he said, as they stepped over the lawn.

Tony had nothing against his father-in-law. He could have had, for Ted had made his disappointment at Susie's choice clear enough. Even at the time, Tony had felt no resentment. It was natural enough that Ted should not be taken with his daughter's selection of a young man with no money and a Scottish accent, whom he suspected also (Tony always thought) of being

Jewish. Ted, in his blazer and RNVR tie, was solid suburban money, even if, or rather perhaps because, he had made none of it himself. There had been a chain of department stores started by his grandfather. Ted had gone to the right sort of Public School for that background, and then to one of the smaller Oxford colleges, then a good war, and then into the family business. It had stagnated in his charge and a dozen years ago or so he had sold out to a larger, more ambitious chain. They had given him a seat on the Board for a couple of years, before easing him into retirement at the age of fifty. Now he golfed in the morning, lunched at the golf-club and piloted his Rover carefully home in the afternoon. He grumbled about the state of the country, and the Unions—'blighters won't work, you know'— but placed some hope in 'that nice little woman who's in charge now. She'll have to go carefully, mind,' he would say. 'You have to go carefully in England.'

He had come to admire Tony, and often quoted him at the golf-club bar.

Now he said, 'worried about Susie', and the ice in his glass tinkled.

This was a bit much. Tony had had a hard day. He liked his garden, and he didn't want to discuss his wife. There was silence, broken only by the chug of their neighbours' lawn-mower.

'She seems, I don't know, unsettled,' Ted said. 'Nothing wrong between you, is there?'

'Wrong? We've been married fifteen years.'

'Seventeen,' Ted said, 'Eddie's fifteen.'

'Yuh,' Tony took a swig of his whisky, laid his glass on a garden bench, lit a cigar.

He was tempted, but the tradition of secrecy he had inherited from his own father was too strong. You didn't talk about your feelings, not your emotional life. This wasn't for the English reason: that such talk might be embarrassing, bad manners, poor form, a sort of constraint that anyway belonged to Ted's generation and was going out of fashion. Tony's reluctance went deeper. You kept that sort of stuff in a dark cave, and guarded the entrance. To admit an outsider was to expose yourself, to give him a weapon to use against you. He looked at his big, olive-coloured hands, with the black hair growing thick on them and the solidity of his gold signet ring. He trusted his hands; they were made for shaping whatever they encountered.

So he said only; 'Susie's all right. She gets fancies.'

'These fancies . . .'

Tony had had to adjust. He was a man of the time, yes, even of the moment, who could sniff the direction of the breeze, and tack accordingly. But his alertness was rooted in distrust, and that distrust in inherited experience. You kept your secrets. He had adapted, yes, to a world where women were allowed a life beyond the confines of the family, but he didn't believe in that world. He didn't respect it. He kept quiet, or fairly quiet, about that. He kept his secrets, even from Freddy, hence the suggestion that Susie came from nowhere, that she had no background, no parents that intruded. And most of the time Ted didn't intrude. Tony knew he had conquered Ted, and he liked him, up to a point anyway, even if he couldn't respect him. That wasn't altogether true either: he respected Ted in an odd unsatisfied manner, for possessing virtues, qualities, which he didn't have himself and which he didn't want to have. They were qualities which were beyond him; beneath him too, if you looked at it another way.

He was surprised that Ted was worried, that he had noticed anything; but then Susie had always been Daddy's girl.

'She hasn't said anything, has she?'

'No, no, Susie never complains.'

That was true, he admitted, where Ted was concerned. Where Ted was concerned, Susie also kept things hidden. Ted was required to think her happy, successful, in charge. Doubts mustn't be allowed to impair his admiration for his daughter.

So, instead of talking about Susie, Tony began to tell

Ted about the problems relating to the Aylesbury development. He gave him a light, edited version.

'Bloody bureaucrats,' Ted said. 'But I think the little woman'll sort them out.'

'Maybe,' Tony said. He had no faith in politicians. That distrust was also inherited. He knew that the State was your enemy, against which you had to conspire and struggle.

A family of fallow deer, shadow-dappled, slipped out of the birch wood to drink at the loch. The buck watched as the others drank, dainty as ballerinas. Fiona and Caro also watched, from the fishing-hut across the angle of the water. Fiona laid her hand on Solomon's rising birse. 'Good dog, good dog.' When the does had drunk their fill, the buck dipped his head to the water, moonlight glistening on the sharp-pointed horns. A streak of moonlight lay like a ribbon spread over the water. The leaves rustled in the soft breeze and, from the meadow beyond the wood, to which the deer would return to graze, a barn owl screeched.

'I love these woods at night, and the deer. . . . On a summer night like this, after rain.'

Fiona's voice was low, but the buck lifted his head, held it suspended, satisfied himself there was no danger, for the fishing-hut was down wind from the drinking-place. Then something—Fiona could not know what—startled a doe. She threw her head up, whisked around, and galloped into the bracken, followed by the others. The girls listened till the sound died away, and there was silence. Fiona stroked the velvet of Solomon's ear.

'Good dog, good boy.'

'Thank you,' Caro said.

'For what?'

'For suggesting we came down. It's years since . . . so different from New York.'

'I couldn't live without it. I don't mean just the deer, but all this. The peace, the night, the woods, it's a sort of enchantment. Will you go back?'

'Not yet. Let's wait a bit.'

'No, I meant to New York.'

'I don't know. It's such a jungle. And PR: I'm good at it, but there's something shabby, false, about the whole thing. It's odd. Americans prize sincerity above everything, and yet their whole culture is founded on insincerity.'

'All those people. I couldn't stand it.'

A trout jumped, taking a night-fly. The air was warm, still moist after the rain. The girls sat in silence. There was a scent of roses from the bush that trailed over the fishing-hut. It mingled with the smell of water, rushes and wet leaves. Solomon shifted his head and laid it on Fiona's foot. She felt his warmth pressing on her ankle.

Fiona said: 'I used to be afraid of the night, and the woods at night. Now I love them.'

'You've changed,' Caro said.

'How?'

'Lots of ways. I didn't like you much, you know. You seemed so certain, disapproving. . . . I don't know . . .'

'Stuck-up?'

'Yes, stuck-up.'

'Oh dear.'

'Not now. I've changed too.' Caro said. 'In important ways.'

She slipped her arm round her sister-in-law, and drew Fiona's head towards her and kissed her, first on the cheek, and then, finding no resistance, on the lips. It was a long, sweet, soft kiss and for a moment the two women held together. Then Fiona drew her head back.

'No,' she said.

'Yes, Fi, please, why not? There's nothing nasty, not between women.' She drew Fiona's head down again, and kissed her hair, burying her lips in the tresses and murmuring words Fiona could not hear. . . . Solomon pressed harder against Fiona's legs, and again she drew away from Caro's embrace.

'Is this something you learned in New York?'

'It's something I learned about myself in New York. Yes.'

She stroked Fiona's cheek, ran her finger along the line of her lips, felt resistance seem to soften, then renew itself.

'Why not?' Caro said. 'You're not happy. I can see that. And I don't like to see you not happy. Beauty in distress,' she said. 'It's all right. I'm laughing at myself, not at you. Beauty in distress and me the knight errant . . .'

Fiona clutched her hand, drawing it away from her lips.

'No, Caro, but no. . . .'

'You don't love Gavin. . . .'

'No. . . .'

'Did you ever?'

'Sort of. Once, maybe. Now I'm not even sure that I'm fond of him. He's let me down so often, one way or another. But no, not this. . . . I'm sorry.'

'Are you shocked, offended? Disgusted?'

Fiona got to her feet, dislodging Solomon. She leaned on the rail, looking at the water and the moonlight play on it, and the shadows cast by the trees.

'I don't know. I always have been. Disgusted, I mean. By the idea. In theory. It's not me. It hadn't occurred to me that it might be you.'

'And now you know. Does that change things?'

She came and stood beside Fiona and, very lightly, laid her arm round her shoulders.

'I hope not, Fi,' she said. 'I couldn't bear it. But then in the other way I hope it might change things. . . .'

'If we're quiet the deer might come back. No, there's the owl again. I don't know, Caro. The telephoning man. He's coming for the week-end . . .'

Caro withdrew her arm, sat down on the bench that ran round the little verandah of the hut, lit a cigarette.

'I see.'

'I don't know that you do. I don't know that I do myself. Give me a cigarette, will you?'

'You don't smoke.'

'No, but give me a cigarette. He's an old friend, the telephoning man. That's all.'

'Is it?'

Fiona drew in smoke, held her hand before her, watched it tremble in the moonlight.

'Is it?' Caro said again.

'It was more once. I haven't seen him in years . . .'

'Well, just remember.' Caro's voice was light. 'I love you. Silly, isn't it?'

Fiona had no reply. There was nothing she could think of to say that was in any way the right thing to say.

'I don't know what he wants,' she said at last, and tossed her cigarette into the water, like the lie from her lips. 'Let's go back.'

At the moment where the path from the woods opened on to the rough grass below the lawn, she turned and took Caro in her arms and kissed her, once, lightly, but like a sister. Then she stepped away.

'It's those woods,' she said. 'They really are enchanted.'

'No,' Caro said. 'But I see what you mean, all the same.'

Tony Lubbock saw his wife change as the lights of her parents' Rover disappeared round the corner of the azaleas. He saw the animation of the evening flee from her, and her mouth turn thin, narrow, discontented. He left her looking after the departing car, and went through to the drawing-room and poured himself another brandy and clipped the end off his third cigar since dinner.

'You can't really mean that you are not going to be here for Eddie's leave-out.'

'Sorry. Told you I have to be in Scotland. Business.'

'Business. I suppose you think I'm a fool.'

'Have it your own way. You and Eddie can manage fine. You can tell him what a shit I am.'

VI

'There's only one thing,' Kat said. 'No bonking.'

They were in a Chinese restaurant. The debris of the meal lay between them. Kenneth tried to retrieve a piece of duck that lay on the table-cloth, but his chopsticks slid around it. Kat picked it up in her fingers and held it out towards him.

'Do you really want it?'

She stretched over and put it between his lips, and then poured two cups of green tea.

'They probably accept that I sleep with people, but they wouldn't like me to at home. Do you understand?'

He wondered if he was surprised. He didn't know. The truth was that he knew very little about other people, and how they thought and so on. He wasn't sure he even knew what he had read. This uncertainty, for which he had long reproached himself, made it seem even more unlikely to him that someone as definite as Kat, someone so sure that she knew what she wanted, should have attached herself to him. He knew what she gave him; he didn't see that he gave her anything that lots of other chaps wouldn't have been happy to give, and would give as well and satisfyingly. Now he saw a moment of uncertainty in her too, read doubt in her eyes. He couldn't know whether it was there because she was doubtful of how her parents would receive him, was afraid even of their judgement, or whether she doubted him, feared even that this condition would cause him to shy off. She was looking at him and not smiling.

'That's fine,' he said. 'But there's something else. You know in the punt,'—he put his fingers to the cup but it was too hot to lift—'when you asked me if I would like you to be a boy, what did you mean?'

'Oh, I don't know. It just came to me, that's all.'

'But you must have meant something.'

'Maybe I did. But I don't know what. It was just an idea.'

'Well, I prefer you as a girl.'

'Good.'

'Was it some sort of test?'

'No, it just came to me. I'm not depraved, not kinky. I just wondered, suddenly. What it would be like, I suppose, and if you would like it. It's not worth making a fuss about.'

'I'm not making a fuss. I certainly don't want to make a fuss. I've just been thinking about it, that's all.'

'You haven't changed your mind.'

'No, I told you just now. It's fine you being a girl. I'll let you know of course if things change.'

'Will they?'

'Can't see why they should.'

They drank their tea, happy to be together, but at the same time with a certain sadness as at the ending of things. It was the last night they would be in Cambridge, in just this relationship. Kenneth would come back next year when Kat would still be up, but it wouldn't be the same. He felt exposed, like a man on the run who suddenly emerges from the woods into open country.

'So that's fine,' she said. 'Do we have to go to Rashid's party?'

'I said we'd look in. There'll be people there I ought to say goodbye to.'

'There's something creepy about Rashid.'

'It's just that we don't know which he prefers, Tony or Toni,' for the twins who had played Viola and Sebastian had absurdly been christened Antony and Antonia.

'Well, which does he?'

'Tony,' he said, not knowing which he meant.

'No, I think it's Toni. All these stage people,' she said. 'They're so phoney.'

'Or Tony?'

They laughed and kissed, lightly, across the table, and were happy, but Kenneth felt shadows lengthen as he called for the bill.

Mr and Mrs Aitken were shy of their daughter. Their pride was evident, and their love of course, but they couldn't quite understand how a girl of theirs had turned out so different.

'She never had any doubt that Cambridge was for her.'

Mr Aitken stacked a dish carefully. Kenneth dried a glass. He had been surprised when Mr Aitken said after supper, 'We'll do the washing-up, shall we?'

'I like washing-up,' Mr Aitken said. 'I've never wanted a dishwasher. Of course we don't really need it, just the two of us. Not even when Kathy's here.'

'Kathy', Kenneth thought, seemed to refer to a different person. Perhaps that was fair enough. Maybe everybody changed when they went home. Except him; but then home was different, with no parents.

'I would never have thought of Cambridge myself. It wasn't the sort of thing considered in my case. But Kathy was saying, or rather I gather from what she was saying, that it would have been natural, almost automatic, in your case, Kenneth.'

'I was lucky to get in. I don't think it's natural or automatic for anyone now.'

'But you'd have felt it unfair if you hadn't.'

Kenneth was happy to leave it there.

'She's ambitious, you know, Kathy.' Mr Aitken held a glass bowl to the light to make sure that he had removed the last traces of the pasta it had contained.

'I was never ambitious. Nor was her mother. I've never thought of that sort of ambition as a good thing. It was suggested that I put in for a headmastership, but I said, "Why should I? I like teaching. I don't like administration. I don't like power." They couldn't understand that, but it seemed to me, still seems, that if you're a teacher and have something to contribute as a

59

teacher, then it's a mistake, an evasion of responsibility, to leave the chalk-face. Good teaching's the most important part of school, and that's what Sheila and I try to do.'

'I like your father.'
  'Really?'
  'Really.'

He felt of course gratitude to him—for having made Kat possible. But it was more than that. Mr Aitken was a good man, not a term which Kenneth naturally found himself applying to people.

They were strolling down the suburban road, to the music of lawn-mowers. The evening was blue-gold and heat still rose from the tarmac. Kenneth had slung a cardigan loose around his shoulders, and felt Kat's arm, cool and warm at the same time, against his. Mr Aitken had suggested they go down to the pub for a pint, and Kenneth was grateful. He was nervous too: there might be friends of Kat's past there, and he wasn't sure how he would cope. He didn't want to risk embarrassing her.

'That's silly,' she said.

'You like it here, don't you?' he said.

'In short doses.'

'But you're keen to leave?'

'I said, "short doses". Look, my mum and dad, they're fine, but they're sort of black-and-white movies, know what I mean.'

'Maybe that's why I like them so much. I'm a bit black-and-white movie too.'

In the morning Mrs Aitken carried Kat off to visit her grandmother. Mr Aitken filled his pipe and read the *Guardian*.

'You would be an old Tory,' he said, 'wouldn't you? You'd be classed as a wet.'

'I'm not a Tory at all. I'm not political.'

'That's right, an old Tory.'

'Are you laughing at me?'

'Just a little. You don't mind, I hope. It's not very

polite. But I don't like this government. Your sort were better. This lot. Well, living here, you know, I've taught people like them. They're all right, in their way, but it's a narrow way. They think private life is all that matters. . . . They think it's all about getting on, that a man's worth is measured by his bank balance. I can't think like that.' He tapped his newspaper with the mouthpiece of his pipe. 'There's a lot of silliness here and I don't agree with a lot of it, but basically, it's on the right side. It thinks there's more to life than material success and it still trusts people to be decent. I've been a teacher for thirty years now, and it gets harder to think that every year, but I still do. I still try. So does Sheila. I'm not sure about Kathy. That's what worries me. But I've been watching you, and listening to you, and I'm puzzled because you don't seem to be setting yourself to be a high-flyer.'

'I'm not. Not at all.'

'But Kathy's obviously very fond of you. So I wonder if I have been misjudging her attitude.'

It wasn't the sort of conversation Kenneth had envisaged. Granted, he wasn't there as a prospective husband, at least he didn't think he was, but he had certainly been brought down, as it were, on approval. And Kat had been nervous in case he displayed social attitudes, prejudices, which would cause that approval to be withheld. But instead of being subjected to inspection, it seemed that he was now to be recruited as some sort of ally: someone who would steer Kat away from the temptations of greed.

It was a sort of privilege, but also disconcerting. Any relationship he had established with Kat's father was tenuous, brittle. This was unknown territory. He had probably never heard the word suburb spoken without a sneer or a laugh. He looked round the trim garden, the neat lawn, the well-ordered hollyhocks, delphiniums and lupins, the weed-free rose-bed. He hadn't been prepared for the sheer niceness, what Kat meant by the black-and-white movie aspect: black-and-white television

61

might be more accurate. He was in a world where people were careful of each other's feelings, where they restrained their egotism to avoid causing disturbance. It was rather attractive.

'Kat's better than the age we live in,' he said, and blushed. It was an absurd remark, even if it was also true.

VII

It was too difficult to remember if she had ever been in love with Gavin. She hadn't married for love anyway. She had seen love and backed away, and never blamed herself for her prudence. So she had married Gavin and made a place for herself, where she fitted in, and was admired. She hadn't thought that was the way a bitch would behave, till Kevin had tried that line with her. But she had resisted; she knew a bitch when she saw one, she had said; that was Diana, her mother, his previous lover, didn't he remember? 'Christ,' he had said, 'you're two of a kind'; but she had formed herself in opposition to Diana, who had embarrassed and frightened and irritated and infuriated her from her thirteenth birthday.

It was a grey morning on the hillside with clouds scudding. The children were mounted. For once neither pony had caused trouble. Now Rosie and Charlie were doing what they loved doing, and what she (rather) loved watching. Only she could scarcely be bothered.

Margot Rutherford, the Pony Club DC, squelched up in wellingtons and riding-mac.

'That man Maconochie. I could wring his neck.'

'What's he done now?'

'I had to disqualify Shuna. Nipper jibbed at a fence, disobedient for two minutes, and Maconochie came up behind and shouted at him till he jumped it. Well, naturally, Sally Ord-Waring, who's judging at that fence, noted "disobedience and outside assistance" on the card, so I disqualified her. Fair enough?'

'Absolutely.'

'Not for Master Maconochie. He has the cheek to tell me that Sally's souwester frightened Nipper. "Maybe it did, my lad," said I, "but if a horse at Badminton takes fright and refuses, it doesn't matter if it was HMQ's headscarf it took exception to. Just too bad".'

'So how did he take that?'

'Swore at me if you please. Got no manners, that lad. His old father was a decent enough soul, but this young one's a counter-jumper.'

'Gavin's been having trouble with him.'

'Gavin's a fool if he leaves his affairs in Master Maconochie's tender care, but then poor Gavin is a fool. No offence, Fiona, you know I always speak my mind. Maconochie's so crooked he shites corkscrews. Ah well, the trials of being a DC. Don't know why I agreed to take the job on again. Had enough trauchle last time to last me. . . . Oh my God, look at that pony with a mouth as full of ironmongery as a sword-swallower. When will folk learn? Rosie going well?'

'Oh yes.'

'And Charlie? I like that boy of yours, he's got spunk.'

As soon as he heard the horse-box drive away, Gavin pushed the papers aside on his desk, looked out of the window to make certain that Fiona had indeed left and that this wasn't some trick being played on him, and got a bottle of Gordon's from the corner cabinet. He sloshed some bitters into the glass, poured a large or largish gin—no more than a pub treble, for it was still early in the day—and added water from the carafe he had already set on the desk. He stood by the window, sipping and watching the clouds, and letting the gin begin to do its healing and calming work.

Fiona never commented on his consumption. She just looked at him. That was worse.

He didn't know what had gone wrong, in any of the several ways things had gone wrong. Some days he found it as hard to look at her as at a bank statement. Maconochie he supposed would have his way. Gavin didn't see how he could resist. He had been brought up to suppose he would always be rich, and now he wasn't.

It had seemed as natural as that the grass should grow, and he didn't understand the process by which he had arrived at his present state of embarrassment. Of course, viewed from outside, which would have required an effort of imagination that was beyond him, he was still very well-off. If he sold up, well, even at the present declining price of land, he was probably worth a million and a half clear. But that wasn't the point. He felt poor, embarrassed, harried. He had reached the point when his man of business looked at him with scorn and said, 'you'll have to sell off this farm to satisfy the bank'.

Last week little Mr Carstairs had telephoned to say, 'I really can't let your overdraft go higher, Sir Gavin. I'll have Head Office on me. I must ask you to keep your cheque-book in your pocket, till you've reduced the balance somewhat.'

Bastards . . . He put down his glass, threw the window up, picked up his shot-gun and fired at a rabbit on the lawn.

He missed. It was that kind of a morning.

'I've always said,' Colin remarked, 'they should reserve the day till the afternoon.'

He scratched Sikes behind the right ear.

'I'm sorry if we're a bit early for you,' Enid Kemsley-Smith flashed teeth at him, 'but I did so want to invite you to dinner tonight, and you weren't answering your telephone and since I happened to be passing . . . well. And something else. What a state you reduced my poor Arthur to! I haven't seen him in such a state since the day he broke eighty at the Royal Mid-Surrey.'

'Ah well, we shall none of us do that again.'

'So you will come to dinner. Do say "yes".'

'Yes.'

'Short notice I know and frightfully rude of me, but in the country you have to act on impulse I find. And my son Rupert is just back from Cambridge. He's dying to meet you.'

'That seems improbable.'

Scamp pecked on landing and Charlie slid over his off-side shoulder. He got to his knees feeling his back, a look of fury on his face. Scamp trotted a few yards and put his head down and began to eat.

'Charlie hasn't a good seat, you know, Mummy,' Rosie said.

Fiona watched her son approach the pony, who lifted his head and trotted off again to resume eating. This game was repeated a few times.

'I suppose I'd better go and help him catch the brute.'

'He'll be disqualified if you do that, Mummy. It doesn't matter because he has so many penalty points anyway. I did well to get clear, didn't I?'

'There are times,' Fiona thought, 'when you remind me too much of myself. Little bitch.'

'Oh good,' she said, 'Caro's caught him.'

'If Scamp does that again,' Charlie said, as they approached, 'he'll go for dog-meat. That's a warning, you silly pony.'

'Did you thank Caro for catching him, dear?'

'I was glad of the exercise,' Caro said. 'It's bloody cold, isn't it. How long is this going to last?'

'Ages, simply ages.'

'Fiona,' Margot Rutherford said, 'that shite Maconochie's gone home in a huff.'

'Good riddance.'

'Yes, but he was down to organize the leading-rein jumping. Will you be a good lass and take over?'

'The joys of motherhood. Charlie, maybe you should pop Scamp over the practice fence. You don't want him to lose confidence.'

'It's not confidence he needs, it's decency. He dropped his shoulder on purpose, Mummy.'

'It's just that you don't have a good seat, Charlie.'

'You shut your face, sister. Come on, dog-meat.'

They galloped into the gathering gloom.

*

When he left the motorway at Perth, Tony Lubbock was in foreign territory. He had been there before of course, as a young man, little more than a boy, invited to dances (in hired kilt, Prince Charlie and lace jabot), and for week-ends when he resolved that one day he would come back to shoot. Well, now, he and Freddy each had a gun in a Hampshire shoot—a syndicate of City men who lunched on game pies from Fortnum's, cheese from Paxton & Whitfield, followed by Kummel, which the organizer of the syndicate insisted was just what was needed if you were to shoot well after lunch. Tony wasn't so sure, but he went along with the ritual. That was all right; he was acclimatized there.

He moved the Mercedes down a gear and turned off the A9. 'There'll be others,' Fiona had said, and then explained that she was sorry, but her week-ends began Saturday afternoon. That was when guests were invited to arrive. 'It works better that way, I've found. Unless there's shooting of course. Then we invite them Friday night, and expect them to leave after lunch on Sunday.'

She had always had that sort of precision, and he was never sure whether it pleased or irritated him.

'You can't go back.' No doubt that was right, if back meant the Ukraine. But beyond that, Tony didn't accept it. His success was based on his Romanticism: the picture he had formed of himself, when he first looked over the narrow twisting streets of the City, and resolved to conquer.

'What sort of chap is he?'

'I've told you, Gavin, I haven't seen him for years.'

That was how she would have had to explain him.

'You're mad,' he said to himself, speaking aloud; and then lit a cigar.

'Chap in a Mercedes. Don't know who. Fi keeps inviting chaps. Don't know from where.'

All right when Bill and Louise had arrived. They were chums, even if not expected by him; Lou the sort of girl

67

you could send to the kitchen to make a pot of tea for herself, and know she wouldn't be offended, nor leave the sort of mess that would upset Mrs Hunter when she returned to do dinner. But unknown chaps in Mercedes!

'Maybe he's got the wrong house. Hope so.'

'So what sort of chap is he?'

Caro's manner hadn't altered on account of the exchanges by the loch last night. It might not have happened, and Fiona was surprised not to find herself thinking differently of Caro.

'It's hard to explain. It's so long ago.'

'Well, was he in love with you?'

'Oh yes.'

'And you?'

'I suppose so.'

'And now?'

'Don't know.'

'Don't know? That means you have a fancy.'

'It's too silly.'

They got the ponies into the box with only token resistance from Scamp, and drove home, through the rain, with wipers working.

She entered, in jeans and baggy sweater, her hair everywhere, and two children shouting to their father. Her cheek was cold when she laid it against his, turning her mouth away from his searching lips.

'So you got here?'

'No problem. Sorry I couldn't make it to your pony do. I like horses, you know. I've got two steeplechasers myself. Get a lot of fun from them even though they don't pay for their keep . . .'

'I backed a winner at thirty-three to one last week,' said Louise.

'Lou's become a habitué of our local betting shop. She scares them stiff.'

'Oh rubbish . . .'

It went on around him, and he was grateful for the chatter. He couldn't take his eyes off her. She pushed a strand of hair away with a mud-streaked hand.

'I'm such a mess, I didn't know you'd taken to gambling, Lou.'

'Like a fish.'

There was a tall dark girl with a crooked jaw, who said: 'So you're the telephoning man. At last.'

She spoke in a low voice so that no one else heard, and with an air of amusement, which he tried to counter.

'And you gave about as little away as the Secret Service.'

They eyed each other.

'What are you anyway?' he said, 'Fiona's bodyguard?'

'Not that, only her sister-in-law.'

And my enemy? But one whom, nevertheless, he set out to charm, to impress with the personality he had learned to display for the purpose of domination. He knew that his charm was formidable, when he chose to exercise it: a string of victories stretched behind him. His hobby (a word he despised), his chief intellectual interest, outside his work, was Napoleon. He collected books about the emperor, paintings, engravings, other memorabilia. He had a lock of his hair which he had bought at an auction in Paris, and carried in a locket made in the shape of the imperial bees. In his own mind his battles were marked off in Napoleonic style; he had fought his Lodi, Marengo, Austerlitz. It was a passion which usually he kept secret, at least in its full intensity, because he sensed it could make him appear ridiculous. Napoleons are, after all, out of fashion.

And this girl was worth fighting, not an aged Austrian archduke disguised as a chinless Old Etonian.

He probed her past. When she mentioned New York, he spoke of the city with authority.

'PR?' he said, 'I used to underestimate PR. Now that I'm, without boasting, in the big league, I've changed my mind. Bad PR can devastate you. All good PR is essentially a matter of avoiding the bad.'

'I'd go further than that,' she said.

'You would?'

And to his surprise found himself telling her about his

difficulties with the Aylesbury development.

'How would you handle that?' he said.

'At the local level. Isolate the Government department.'

'You could be right.'

'Find inconsistencies in their argument, things that don't conform to precedent.'

'My own reaction is to screw them.'

'That's crude. You don't need to be crude surely.'

'I said, my first reaction. But there are times when the direct attack under the belt, is best.'

He'd never accepted that judgement that the seizure and execution of the Duc D'Enghien was 'worse than a crime, a blunder'. Its effectiveness proved it no blunder, and if it was no blunder, then it seemed to him no crime either.

'You know the Roman motto,' he said. '*Oderint, dum metuant*. Let them hate provided they fear.'

'I'm impressed.'

'That I know some Latin? You shouldn't be.'

'No, that you lead trumps so soon.'

'Poker's my game, not bridge.'

'Yes, I can see it would be.'

When they dispersed, to get ready for dinner, it came to him that he had had no word with Fiona. But then she hadn't spoken to her husband either. She had been engaged with the man Bill, who was apparently a surgeon in Edinburgh, and who had been telling her about a house he had bought in Provence, and trying to persuade her to visit them there in September.

'Oh,' she said, 'I haven't been abroad in years, Bill. The dogs, you know.'

And he wondered, being in the frame of mind when every remark is searched for relevance to one's immediate interest, whether those words were meant to convey a warning to him.

VIII

'Well, I must say, you're an oil-painting.'

Liz had brought Rory as well as the decorative Jason. Rory could be called decorative too. He had lately taken to dressing like a Landseer Highlander: big spade beard, kilt, tartan jacket for evening wear.

'It's for the tourists,' he said, 'there's no money in land these days.'

'Nothing to do with the tourists,' Liz said. 'He just fancies himself.'

'It's a cool get-up,' Jason said.

Well, Colin thought, you have picked yourself one here, Liz dear, trouble I would think. But Liz was alert enough to have Master Jason nicely summed up; if he was out for Number One, so was she. And there was something in what Rory said: he represented after all a species that had outlived its utility. He was a Clan Chief, of sorts, and most of his clansmen were in Alberta, Arkansas, or South Island, New Zealand. Or Glasgow, of course. One mustn't forget Glasgow and London. So what was there really for Rory to do but present himself as someone playing a part, an actor who was as amused by his own performance as he expected the tourists to be? Liz and Rory were well-matched, which was why, despite everything, their marriage had endured; they both saw themselves in character roles.

Enid Kemsley-Smith had been busy. You would never think they were barely settled here. The house, which had mouldered in the ownership of a dismal old man called Major Archibald, veteran of several botched military expeditions, had been revitalized.

'Yes,' she said, 'People have always told me I have a flair for houses. Sometimes I think I should have done it professionally.'

'Never too late, old thing,' said her husband.

'Oh no, I'm past that now. I would never have the energy. I'm far too old,' she said, and looked round for contradiction.

'No,' she said, 'I'm ready to put my feet up.'

Arthur busied himself with drinks; he made the pouring of these appear a complicated business.

'So what do you do with yourself all the time, Colin?' she said.

'Very little.'

'If you can find an answer to that question,' Liz said, 'you'll have solved one of the mysteries of the world: how Colin gets through the day.'

'I say,' Arthur pushed a gin-and-tonic at Colin, 'that picture of the Colonel's. Something else, eh?'

'What's this?' Liz said. 'One of Gerry's filthy pictures?'

'I haven't seen it myself, but Arthur can talk of nothing else.'

'One of old Straloch's,' Colin said.

'Dirty old man.'

'Yes, Gerry thinks it's a Wimsey.'

'Wimsey?'

'Wimsey.'

'You don't mean Wimsey?'

'Well, yes I do, that's why I said Wimsey.'

'Who's Wimsey?'

'You must have heard of Wimsey, Rory. Even you.'

'Little business with some Guardsmen in Hyde Park,' Colin said, 'then old Straloch gave him board and lodging when he came out. . . . Not without talent. I quote Gerry. Don't know anything about these things myself, naturally. Who am I to judge whether a painting is well painted? Nice piece of smut though.'

'I'm lost,' Enid said. 'Fill me in.'

She was trembling with what Colin supposed to be excitement. It might have been irritation of course. She wasn't, he guessed, a woman who liked to be out of things. But then which of them did?

'Arthur couldn't make sense of it.'

'Oh sense . . .'

'Well, you explain it.'

Colin was spared the effort however by the arrival of more guests. There were three: a middle-aged lady with brassy hair and brassy manner, and two girls, all unknown to Colin. They were introduced to the company with a certain flourish as Jennifer Prepperton, daughter Angie (a sad mousy creature), and her niece Zoe, tall, red-haired and wildly improbable to Colin's eyes.

'Jenny however,' Enid said, 'will be better known to you all as Ginny Prepper.'

'Not to me,' Colin said, 'but I gather from your tone that she is of some celebrity. It shows yet again that I am sadly out of things. Sikes, I'm afraid, won't have heard of her either.'

The redhead Zoe threw herself on the sofa and began to giggle. She lay on her belly with her heels kicked up and her tartan skirt, which was slit up the side, falling away to reveal an astonishing length of tolerably shapely leg.

'I am here,' Mrs (Ms? Miss?) Prepperton said, 'for research purposes.' She spoke in the rich drawl of the Southern States, agreeable to the ear, but posing problems of comprehension. 'My new novel is significantly set in High Scottish society. . . . My heroine, Amethyst, is the illegitimate daughter of a Scottish duke, torn between love for the son of her father's gamekeeper who is a commodity broker in the City of London, and Dolores, a lovely Creole model with the rapacity of a snake and the morals of an alley-cat.'

'Remarkable.'

'It's already sold to seventeen countries, and Ginny's advance is in seven figures.'

'Lire or pounds?'

'Dollars. I only deal in dollars.'

'Bit out of date,' Liz whispered. 'Be better off in yen . . .'

'Or marks,' Colin said. 'I begin to think I have underestimated Mrs Kemsley-Smith.'

'Zoe, stop giggling,' the bestseller said, without effect.

'We're only waiting for Rupert now,' Enid said. 'The dear boy does so love to make an entrance.'

Across the valley and eight miles away, Fiona was finding it hard to listen to the long dissertation on the state of Scotland with which Bill was treating the dinner-table. Quite how he had embarked on the subject wasn't clear. It seemed to be connected with something Tony Lubbock had said, and Bill was explaining that, though Scotland voted Labour, it wasn't to be thought of as a Socialist country. He voted Labour himself, after all. The thing about Scotland, he was saying, was that Scotland and Scottish culture respected the individual— there was, he insisted, nowhere outside the USA where a surgeon like himself was more highly regarded, for example, not on account of social status, to which Scots were indifferent, but rather, and it was a big but, a very big but, by reason of the respect felt for professional skills; at the same time however there was an equal depth of respect for social communal values, which had been lost, if it had ever existed—and he couldn't be sure that it had—in England.

Bill spoke with great energy. He waved his claret glass at Tony Lubbock, who couldn't divert the flood of conversation without obvious rudeness. Bill's bald red head sweated, as if exuding the claret of which he had already drunk more than a bottle.

'We have no high regard for greed,' he said. 'That's not our way.'

'Bollocks, Bill,' Gavin lifted his gaze from the table-cloth and spoke for the first time in half an hour. His utterance was thick, but there was no doubt as to his meaning.

'Bollocks,' he said again. 'You should meet that young

74

shit Maconochie. He's as greedy as a weasel in a pheasant's nest.'

'Scotland inspires me. We used to come here when I was just a li'l girl, and it inspired me even then. The poetry, the romance, the purple heather . . . why I could just die for Scotland.'

Ginny Prepper's bosom heaved, majestic as the liners on which she had first presumably crossed the Atlantic.

The girl Zoe said:

'Aunty believes in reincarnation. She was Mary, Queen of Scots herself in a former life, weren't you, Aunt?'

'One can never be certain of these things, but I have intimations. When I visited Loch Leven, I was chilled to the marrow. Yes, the marrow.'

'She really is certain,' Zoe said. 'I think reincarnation's junk. I used to think it was dandy. That was when I was a Buddhist.'

Colin, to his surprise, was impressed by the emptiness of her voice. The combination of flat voice and far from flat figure was remarkable. Then he remembered how she had thrown herself on the sofa and giggled.

'But you have a daughter,' he said to the bestseller. 'Mary Stuart had only a son.'

'Things work out different other times round,' she said. 'The great Wheel of Fate throws out strange and diverse patterns.'

'No man can bathe in the same river twice,' Colin said.

'That's cute,' Zoe said.

'Heraclitus. No credit to me.'

'You're Andrew Meldrum's brother, aren't you?'

The young man across the table was addressing him. He opened his eyes very wide when he spoke.

'You know Andrew, do you?'

'Well, we've met.'

Colin looked at him. This was the son of the house, Robin? Rupert? Ruby-lips?

'I suppose you would have,' he said.

He turned back to Zoe.

'When you did believe in reincarnation, a charming but fallacious notion, who were you in previous existence?'

'I dunno. Maybe that's what put me off the idea.'

'I can see it might.'

Tony Lubbock was amazed to see Fiona rise and lead the other ladies from the dining-room, while Gavin fetched a decanter of port from the sideboard. He didn't know such things still happened.

'Oh we like to keep up standards in Scotland,' Bill said.

When the decanter had circulated, Gavin got to his feet again.

'The Queen.'

'D'you know,' Bill said, 'last week, I was at a public dinner, men and women together, that sort of thing, and when the loyal toast was proposed, the lady opposite me sat tight, and said, "don't drink to the lady, got nothing against her personally, but don't drink to her." Extraordinary. Let me see just how deep nationalism runs, when people do that sort of thing at a Charity Dinner.'

'Sods,' Gavin said. 'They're everywhere.' He looked at Tony Lubbock as if seeing him for the first time.

'You're not one yourself, are you?'

'Not what? A sod?'

'Not a bloody Nat, that's what . . .'

'No,' Tony Lubbock said, 'you can't mark that against me.'

'Well, you can't tell nowadays. You can't tell about anything. Push the boat out, will you. Or brandy? Anyone prefer a spot of brandy?'

Tony did, Gavin likewise.

Colin drove home, at twenty miles an hour, keeping to the middle of the road. This allowed him to veer wildly, but comparatively safely, at corners. Fortunately the road was quiet, and drivers in this part of Perthshire were seldom molested by the police.

He sang as he drove:
'Yield not to temptation,
For yielding is sin . . .'

Temptation, Aunt Annie (now confined to a Church of Scotland Old Folks' Eventide Home in Brechin) had always believed, was sexual. Not that she had yielded herself, she would die a virgin. Living in Perthshire she had even escaped rape, as might not have been the case in, say, Glasgow or Notting Hill, where he had once, moons ago, had a garden flat. Temptation as identified by Aunt Annie hadn't come his way much in recent years either.

That made this evening odd. He thought, as he nearly landed himself in the ditch, about undressing the girl Zoe. In his youth, it might have been the matter of a moment. Well, no doubt it still wouldn't take long. That wasn't quite the point.

He stopped the car, peering at a cross-roads, and inched his way forward. Once across, he stopped again, reached into the glove-pocket, extracted a flask, opened it with some difficulty, and took a swig.

Famous Grouse? Probably.

Yes, well . . .

'Cease, Fool,' he said aloud, 'the fate of Gods may well be thine;
Wouldst thou survive the marble or the oak?
When nations, tongues, and worlds must sink beneath the stroke.'

IX

Sunday morning: Tony Lubbock stood by the dining-room window, with a view broken by the stone balustrade that divided the upper lawn from the croquet green and rose-beds below. Mist hung still over the hills. He held his mobile telephone to his ear.

'Well,' he said, 'we can screw him. Thanks, Shane. You've done well. Check on the car number, will you?'

He clicked the cut-off button and slipped the telephone into the inside breast-pocket of his suede jacket. He helped himself to kedgeree from the sideboard.

Caro said: 'I looked into the dining-room. He's on his own. He didn't notice me because he was on the phone.'

'In the dining-room. How could he?'

'Mobile.'

'Mobile? Oh, I see.'

'He's waiting for you.'

'Oh dear, I don't think I like him at all now.'

Fiona dipped the last corner of toast into her cup of Lapsang. Sunday was the one morning she liked to rise late.

'Maybe you should suggest church,' Caro said.

'Oh, I don't suppose he ever goes to church.'

'Bill's still asleep. All that lovely vino. Doesn't seem to have affected you.'

'I like a good breakfast. Do you get the Sunday papers here?'

'Oh sometime, I suppose. I don't know. We're curious about you.'

When Lou was young and pretty she had found the

direct, innocent approach effective. She still employed it, with less success now.

'It's not often Fiona has guests whom she hasn't known for yonks. Not to stay. She's so sweet, do you know her well, we've been friends ever since. Gavin hadn't a clue who you were, didn't even seem to know you were coming, of course he might have forgotten, poor dear's in a bit of a daze these days, gin of course, but I don't think it was that, I think Fi really hadn't told him, which made little me curious. . . .'

He didn't reply, forked kedgeree into his mouth.

'She's so sweet, and she used to be really good at entertaining people, but I don't know, the poor darling seems to have lost her edge. . . .'

Fiona was nervous of course. She had been railroaded by him and now she didn't know how to react. Well, he could handle that, if she gave him the chance. All he needed was half-an-hour, without this chatter, and they would be up and running.

Sunday morning, cafard heavy as the mist. Colin, alone of those who had been at either dinner-party, would attend church. He had taken to doing so in the last year, marching down the avenue to the Episcopalian chapel half a mile beyond the gates. Sikes accompanied him, though Sikes did not attend divine service. Colin shut him up in the shed where the lawn-mower was kept. Sikes slept on a pile of empty sacks while Colin intoned the General Confession. 'We have erred and strayed from thy ways like lost sheep . . . but thou, O Lord, have mercy upon us, miserable offenders, spare thou them, O God, who confess their faults, Restore thou them that are penitent. . . .' He liked the words. That was why he went there. They reminded him of school, when, remarkable as it now seemed, he had known penitence. At the age of fifteen he had even attended extra Lenten services. Once, during the General Confession, he had seen Mansie Niven slip his hand under another boy's kilt and (presumably) squeeze the thigh, stroke the bottom.

'You should have had your eyes shut,' Mansie had said, 'I always keep my eyes shut when I pray.'

There were no hymns at St Ninian's. A congregation of five, which was a slightly above average turn-out, sounded silly singing hymns.

But Colin sang as he marched up the avenue after the service:

'We plough the fields and scatter
The good seed on the land;
But it is fed and watered
By God's almighty hand . . .'

A car drew up:

Enid Kemsley-Smith leaned out of the window.

'You are an early bird.'

It seemed he had invited them for a drink, though he had no memory of doing so. He had promised to show Zoe the stuffed peacock. It was rum: her enthusiasm, Mrs Kemsley-Smith said, knew no bounds. But the bird was only briefly admired, then forgotten.

Zoe wore midnight-blue cycling shorts, open-toed sandals and a soft creamy jersey. Her Titian hair was piled high, the jersey was loose and V-necked, revealing an amplitude of neck, shoulders and just a hint of breast. She held the eye longer than the peacock had done.

Sikes sniffed, in seeming disapproval, at the ankles of the boy Rupert, who was made uncomfortable by the dog's attentions.

'He sometimes bites my brother Andrew,' Colin said; which wasn't in fact true since Andrew had not visited Colin during the bull-terrier's lifetime.

'He has superb judgement,' Colin said, as the dog shifted his attentions to Zoe and began to lick her calf.

'I always say,' Enid Kemsley-Smith said, 'that there's nothing to beat a Sunday morning drink.'

She downed her gin-and-It and held out her glass.

'Such a jolly night,' she said. 'Ginny's my oldest friend, you know. Don't be deceived by her accent. That was carefully acquired.'

80

'Gee, yes,' Zoe spoke for the first time. 'When she married my uncle, Colonel Prepperton, she jus' fell in love with li'l old Mississippi.'

'We were in the chorus-line together,' Enid said. 'That was before I met Arthur. Dearest Rup gets his artistic sensibility from me. Ginny comes from Weybridge actually, she's my oldest and dearest friend. I do like a girl who gets on in the world.'

'Up to a point,' Colin said, regarding Zoe, who had subsided on the tiger-skin rug (a trophy of Great-Uncle Matthew's days in Skinner's Horse) and started to giggle again.

'Get up, Zoe,' Enid said. 'Anyone would think you were retarded.'

'Surely not.'

'Southern belle,' Rupert said; nastily, Colin thought.

Zoe continued to giggle and kicked her heels in the air. Sikes began to lick the backs of her legs just below the cycling shorts.

He lay down beside her and licked industriously; it was clear to Colin, expert student of the thought-processes (for want of a better term) of bull-terriers, that Sikes had recognized a soul-mate.

Mrs Kemsley-Smith began to talk of her plans for what she called the summer season. They seemed to involve Colin heavily. On the other hand, it appeared that the Preppertons would be with her for some time also.

'Ginny's just drinking up background. She adores research. And then of course dearest Rup looks just like Lord Darnley. That excites her, she says it deepens her understanding of Mary.'

'The handsomest long man that ever I did see,' Zoe said. 'That's what she says.'

By noon Fiona had still made no appearance. Tony Lubbock had endured the conversation first of Lou, then of Bill, with an ill-grace that did not seem to transmit a message to them. Bill had talked for some time of concepts of social responsibility inherent in the Scottish character.

'We have faults. I don't deny that,' he said, 'but the vulgar pursuit of self-interest isn't one of them. There's a stout Presbyterian residue of feeling even if formal faith has lapsed. I recognize it in myself: the work-ethic directed at social goods.'

He continued in this vein for some twenty minutes.

He hovered on the lawn.

Caro said: 'you really must put him out of his misery. I'm beginning to feel quite sorry for him.'

'He's got this idea, that's all,' Fiona said. 'It's got nothing to do with me. I think I'll have another snooze.'

'Oh dear, that's Gavin joining him now. Should I rescue him?'

'As you like. . . .'

'You're a money man, I gather.'

'Could put it like that.'

'Do all right, do you?'

'Well enough, can't complain.'

'Don't understand money myself.' Gavin scratched his moustache. 'Goes up and down of its own accord, seems to me. You work away, just as usual, and all of a sudden, things have changed. All this . . . you see . . .' he waved to indicate the extent of the estate, now bathed in a watery sunshine. 'Just came to me. Seemed all right. Now they tell me it isn't.'

'Who tells you?' Tony's lethargy slipped away. This was his own territory. 'Who tells you?'

'My man of business, Maconochie he's called. Shortage of liquidity, he says. Got to sell a farm to get liquid capital. That make sense to you?'

'Liquidity does. Way things are going to be, cash is the thing to be in. You can take that from me.'

'Cash, eh?' Gavin nodded, impressed. 'How can you be in cash though, either have it or don't, I'd have thought.'

'Keep your money in cash, that's what I mean.'

'Money in cash, eh? I see. No, I don't. I'm fogged. Trouble is, you see, don't have cash to be in. Short of

82

cash. That's what. That's why Maconochie—young shit—tells me to sell this farm. Least, think that's why . . .'

'Do that,' Tony Lubbock screwed up his eyes, 'and I would ask who's buying. Might be your Maconochie himself. Might have plans for the land himself. Thought of that . . ?'

'Maconochie, young shit. Don't want to sell the farm.'

'All the same, you want cash, don't you?'

'Oh yes, want cash.'

They took a turn around the lawn.

'They're very deep in conversation,' Caro said.

'Poor Tony. Serves him right.'

'I've got a proposition,' Tony said. 'Keep the farm. Sell your wife.'

'Fiona? Sell Fiona? Joking. Who'd buy?'

'I would.'

'You? You would? But chaps don't buy and sell wives. Not Arabs you know. Not done.'

'Why not? You want cash, I'll buy Fiona from you.'

'Joking. That why you came here?'

'You could say so . . .'

'Joking.'

'Sure,' Tony said, 'joking. But when you think of it, wives are a commodity, and a damned expensive one. No reason why they shouldn't be bought and sold.'

'Well, I must say . . . Gin-time, eh? Talked about this to Fiona . . .?'

'Nuh-huh, solve your liquidity problem.'

'Just isn't done, old boy.'

'Could be done.'

'Aunt Ginny says it's her duty to bring Romance into people's narrow lives. Guess I don't believe in duty.'

Enid Kemsley-Smith and Rupert had departed to lunch with Mansie Niven. It seemed that Zoe was not included in the invitation. It seemed also that it was assumed that he, Colin, would be happy to entertain her. Certainly, she had continued to recline on the tiger-skin while he showed the others out.

'Or Romance?' he said.

'Shit, no.'

That was reassuring. She was a strange girl. Unusually, Colin felt he had been wrong-footed, matters not arranged to his convenience. He set limits to encounters, conducted them on his own terms. Now he was challenged, simply because this girl didn't seem to want anything. She wanted anything even less than he did, that was the trouble. Or was it? Did she really want him? Surely not. People didn't. That was an article of the tattered creed by which Colin contrived to lead his life.

You stayed detached. What, though, if you encountered someone who was even more detached . . ?

'I've never read your aunt's books,' he said.

'They're junk.'

'Actually I'd never heard of her.'

'That's OK.'

'You don't seem to have much time for her.'

'So?'

'So why do you travel round with her?'

Round One to her; he had displayed curiosity.

'So: why not?'

'Well,' he said, baffled. 'Well, some people might say . . .'

But it was no good. He had no idea of what some people might say. They might after all say anything. People did. When you turned on the television and they gave you a snatch of what he believed television people called 'vox pops', the responses were of an infinite variety, sometimes well-expressed, sometimes of course quite incomprehensible.

'I've no idea,' he said. 'Other people are a mystery to me.'

Fiona did not descend to lunch, which consisted only of cold meats and pickles. Caro explained that she had a headache, was keeping to her bed.

'Hopes she'll be down in time to say good-bye.'

'Poor love,' said Lou, helping herself to a wedge of salmon.

'Hope you don't mind my saying so,' Bill said, 'but what goes on in the City of London offends Scots morality. We don't like to see people's jobs being bought and sold. I don't say a job's property . . .'

'Good.'

'But it's a precious jewel. Do you chaps ever think of the consequences of your actions?'

'Yes,' Tony Lubbock said. 'We think how bloody nice to throw a couple of thousand more sods in Lanarkshire on the scrapheap. That makes our day, gives us an appetite for dinner, puts zest in the martini, that kind of thing.'

'That's a bit rough.'

'You talk balls, do you know that? You forget, or maybe you don't know, I was brought up in Edinburgh myself. There's nothing you can tell me about the stupid snobbery and hypocrisy of them there. That's your Scots morality—fur coat and nae knickers.'

In the cavernous kitchen, where cobwebs hung in the corners and a yew tree had spread across the window, rendering the light perpetual November, Colin put a packet of oatcakes, a hunk of Cheddar, a jar of pickled walnuts, a tub of herring in sour cream, on a tray with plates and glasses. He fetched a bottle of claret and a corkscrew, and then carried lunch back up to the study where he lived the greater part of his waking hours. Zoe still lay with Sikes on the tiger-skin.

'You do eat, don't you?'

'Uh-huh.'

'I could feed you there, but Sikes will take it.'

She got to her feet in one smooth, unhurried, Venus-from-the-waves movement, and joined him at the table. She turned her chair round so that she sat astride it as if on a horse, and leaned her arms on its back and looked at him.

*

'You got pretty rough with Bill.'

'Man's a fool.'

'Sure.'

Tony Lubbock was finding it difficult to keep pace with Caro. He had been surprised when she suggested a walk, then, guessing she was an emissary from Fiona, accepted. She had set off up the hill towards the moors at a long hill-walking stride. Two spaniels rushed ahead investigating the scrub at the side of the path, and then the heather, as they emerged out of the pines into open country. Tony Lubbock was panting hard and sweating. It annoyed him that the girl seemed unaffected by the exercise.

'In New York,' she said, 'the business geniuses, the top-notchers, drink Perrier and don't smoke.'

'Sure, and they eat health foods and die of ulcers. I'm different.'

'They'd call you old-fashioned.'

He sat on a broken wall and took out his cigar case, clipped a cigar and lit it, blowing smoke towards her.

'*And* you're what Fiona would call chippy,' she added.

He drew deep on his cigar. This girl couldn't know what cigars meant to him; his poor father had always bought himself a box of twenty-five Romeo y Julietta for Christmas. It was his only indulgence and he smoked one every second Sunday throughout the year. Tony had never been able to understand why the old man didn't treat himself to two boxes and a cigar every week. At last, aged eighteen, he had asked him, and his father replied: 'every Sunday I have no cigar I remember there were years when I thought I should never smoke a cigar again. So the Sundays I have a cigar it tastes very good.' Tony had once had a secretary who complained that he spent more than her salary on cigars. He had raised her, but the raise had still fallen short of his cigar expenditure. This girl, Caro,—he looked at the nose-tilted profile—wouldn't like that story. So he told it her. Then he said:

'Did Fiona suggest you took me for this walk?'

'No, why should she? I just wanted to prevent you from murdering Bill.'

'He's not worth it. So you don't have a message for me?'

'Not from Fiona. . . .'

'You don't like me?'

'I don't know you. I don't like the type you present yourself as.'

'Too bad. Fiona's the only woman I've ever loved. I lost her once. I'm not going to lose her again.'

'Who do you think you are? Clark Gable? Humphrey Bogart? Gary Cooper?'

'D'you think I'm awful?'

Zoe stretched out her fingers and took a herring from the tub and popped it whole in her mouth.

'Not a fair question,' Colin said. 'I didn't think you'd eat herring.'

'I used to be a vegan. It got too boring. Why's it not a fair question?'

'Sikes likes herring too. Give him one. Well, for one thing it's not a fair question because if I thought you were awful I probably wouldn't answer. And for another, it's the sort of question which is usually intended to elicit a protest, that you're not awful, you're marvellous or terrific. And for a third thing, it's a boring question because obviously if I thought you were awful I wouldn't be giving you lunch, if you count this as lunch. So there's no way of answering it. But I'll tell you this: I once saw a girl, a black girl in a Roman suburb, who was wearing a T-shirt with the legend, "How can We Lose When We're So Sincere?" It was the time of Vietnam, and I thought "easily, you poor silly. . . ." Well, I don't think you'd wear such a T-shirt.'

'I can't stand slogans on T-shirts.'

'So what can you stand?'

'Well, that's kinda the question, I was sort of hoping you would answer for me . . .'

'My dear girl, how can I?' Colin poured more wine and picked up his glass and drank. 'Bull-terriers obviously. That's a point in your favour certainly. . . .'

'I don't get a kick outa sex. Aunt Ginny thinks that's bizarre. But I just don't, not since I was thirteen.'

She wore a look of ineffable silliness. Colin began to think she was perhaps rather intelligent. Well, in the days when he was interested in girls, he had never been able to decide whether silly girls were more trouble than intelligent ones or vice versa. . . .

'That was when Uncle Prepperton first made to rape me.'

'Didn't succeed?'

She shook her head.

'Guess he lost interest half way through. He lost interest real easy. That's why he went bankrupt so often and why Aunt Ginny took to writing novels if you call them novels she does.'

Caro lay in the sun which was now hot and talked about Fiona. She lay on her side, propping up her head with her left hand, and chewed a blade of grass as she spoke. She explained Fiona's fears, inhibitions, her strong sense of duty. She didn't mention Kevin, though one night Fiona had told her about that business and about what it had revealed to her of her own nature. Talk of Kevin would give Tony Lubbock the idea that she might be available, and it was Caro's intention to make it clear that she wasn't. So she described Fiona's place in the family, talked of the brilliance, as it had once seemed, of Colin and Belinda—'they really seemed too glamorous to me when I was a child'—and about Andrew and his ambitions, and then about their mother, Diana, and how her example had horrified and frightened Fiona. So that was why Fiona had married Gavin, because she needed security and though Gavin himself was a poor fish, he brought security with him.

'I made him an offer,' Tony said.

'What do you mean?'

'For Fiona. I made him an offer.'

'You're mad.'

'He's considering it.'

'You're not only mad. You're disgusting. I bet you've got a wife yourself too.'

'Course I have. Not for much longer though. Doesn't matter. It wasn't a swap I offered him. Cash down.'

'But you can't buy and sell people.'

'It's what I do. You heard that fool, Bill.'

Then he smiled. She felt his charm. She was immune to it, of course. When she had made that crack about Gable & Co, the scorn was real. But now she sensed how Tony would be attractive to women who were attracted by men. There were men of course that she'd been attracted by, but they weren't this type. Before New York had changed her, or rather, as she preferred to put it, released her, she had gone through a succession of relationships with wimps, men who lacked self-confidence and wanted a woman to tell them what to do, drive them on. She was in those days happy to oblige, and that willingness caused her pain in the long run. Usually, though, she was bored before the pain arrived. She could see how Fiona might respond to Tony. She understood why she was afraid to be alone with him, even though she also judged that Fiona was sincere when she said, 'Oh dear, I don't think I like him at all'. Liking, Caro thought, didn't come into it.

Now Tony was talking of his youth, when he had loved and lost Fiona.

'I blamed her for years,' he said. 'I really hated her. She had chickened out, and that's the worst thing you can do, I've always believed that. You have to see what you want and grab it. That's my philosophy. All right, you don't like it, I can see that in your expression, but I add this: and then take the consequences.'

'Isn't that what you're not doing?' she said.

'What do you mean?'

'Well, you went your way. Fiona couldn't go with you. You lost her. Now you're trying to dodge the consequence of your decision, your choice, by going back. . . .'

Tony didn't answer. He drew on his cigar and looked to the mountains that loomed northward. One of the spaniels lay panting beside him, and he tickled her behind the ear.

'You'll only make her unhappy,' she said, 'Fiona, not the dog. If you really cared for her, you'd go away, but you don't care for her,' she said. 'You want her. That's all. Like a company you tried to take over that escaped you and you're still chasing.' She paused, 'You frighten her,' she added.

'Balls,' he said, still fondling the spaniel. 'She was frightened before I came back into her life. I saw her sitting in the NB and she would have looked dead if she hadn't looked scared. So it's not me, it's herself. She's got all this and she sees it was a rotten bargain. . . .'

'Don't forget the children. She adores them.'

'Mother-love,' Tony Lubbock said. 'That's the ultimate cheat isn't it? They grow up, and these days the mother is still young, still a woman, when they do that. . . . It's a bear market, mother-love. . . . You can make money in a bear market, course you can, but only if you know what you are doing. The poor girl hasn't a clue.'

'Rosie's only ten,' she said, 'or is it eleven?'

Zoe had returned to the tiger-skin, Sikes beside her. She stretched out her legs against the rough fur of the rug.

'When I dropped out of college, they sent me to a psychiatrist,' she said, 'he told me I was crazy about myself, specially my body. I guess he was right.'

'Well, it's a nice body.'

'Oh sure. He said I was so crazy about myself that I couldn't be crazy about anyone else. I was so crazy, he said, I didn't want to make a single move in any direction. I was so crazy, that was why I thought everyone else thought I was awful. Nobody could be as crazy about me as I was. I guess he was a good psychiatrist, but he wasn't much help. Maybe he was a rotten one, I don't know.'

'Psychiatrists talk junk. I shouldn't brood on it.

Besides, self-love's the only one that never lets you down. I'm an expert on the subject. . . .'

She wasn't listening. She would never listen. Colin might be able to say all the things he only said when he was alone and they would stay hidden, because she wouldn't listen. Only, she might; you could never tell what egotists latched on to, or how they would take whatever they chose to hear. You could be sure of one thing of course; in some manner they would annex it, make it their own. Still, she was nice to look at. During a conversation in the City & County, a club where there was no tiresome convention about not discussing ladies, Gerry had once said, 'I think I feel my annual erection coming on'. Colin's were more frequent, still rare enough to surprise him these days.

Zoe said: 'Who's this guy they've gone to lunch with? They were both quite excited.'

'Mansie, he's an old chum. To employ an ancient formula, he's a very ugly man and not half as nice as he looks. He's a Member of Parliament, for what that's worth, not a lot in my opinion. You can't take him seriously. Even Mansie can't take himself altogether seriously.'

'Bo-ring. Your brother's a Member of Parliament too, Rup says. Rup says he made a pass at him.'

'Well, looking at the boy, I don't suppose the pass was dropped.'

'My psychiatrist suggested I try a lesbian relationship. Bo-ring.'

'Look, I'm not asking a lot.'

'Oh yes, you are,' Caro said.

But really she was puzzled.

It was late afternoon, with the sun still high and hot, but it was cool and dark in the woods through which they were now passing on their way back to the house. The trunks of the pine trees were streaked pink and gold, and a smell of damp and decay pervaded the air around the folly which Gavin's grandfather had built, to his

91

wife's displeasure, in honour of an Edwardian version of the God Pan. Pan wasn't doing well; he had lost his nose and the roof of his temple was broken.

'Smells like a dead deer,' Caro said. 'I bet Lucy rolls in it. She's got a passion for that and she really stinks afterwards. It's a pity we didn't bring a lead.'

Tony Lubbock sat on the steps of the temple and lit another cigar.

'I've been trying to work it out,' he said. 'You fancy her yourself, don't you?'

'I don't know what that's got to do with you,' Caro said.

'Not a lot,' he smiled.

His composure irritated her as much as his perception. She hadn't looked for either in him. She sat down beside him on the temple steps, and leaned forward, elbows on thighs, hands dangling, looking down as if she was examining the moss that grew around the base of the building.

'But it's true, isn't it?' he said.

'I don't have to answer that.'

'Know the first rule about being interviewed?' he said. 'If you're asked a question and you say you don't have to answer it, you've answered it. I once saw an MP on the telly—a Tory of course—and it was a late night show and the interviewer said to him, "Are you gay", and course he said, "I don't have to answer that question", and all the forty-seven sods who were watching at that time of night immediately saw him picking up rent boys in Leicester Square. So OK, and I see that puts you against me, but I can't think you stand a chance.'

'It's not like that,' she said.

'Isn't it? All right I'm wrong, and you're just the faithful second lead with a shoulder to cry on. By the way, I'm not prejudiced. One of the best analysts I ever had working for me was a Lizzie. I was really sorry when I had to get rid of her.'

'Oh,' she said, 'and why did you have to do that?'

'She upset the other girls in the office. They complained of sexual harassment.'

There was all at once that mood. Men who only a couple of months back called for another bottle of Heidsieck in wine bars at five in the afternoon were now looking at their watches, and sinking a couple of fast gins before taking the train home. There they unwrapped, as it were, their latest purchases and wondered if they had been fools to make them. The mood of confidence which had held them rapt was loosening its grip. Even Freddy was joining the doubters. Only yesterday, he had told Tony that he didn't see how it could go on. Now he clutched at the Aylesbury deal as if losing that would lose them everything.

'Times is tough,' Tony said. 'But times has been tough before. Don't get your knickers in a twist. Worse things happen at sea.'

Tony didn't like defeatism. Freddy was going soft. Freddy didn't understand. In his heart Freddy believed that life was there to support him. Tony was his father's son. He had behind him memories of expropriation, disaster striking from dark clouds, a hostile State; he knew that no matter how high you soared you could never be certain of cigars next year.

Aylesbury was important, sure. He knew that as well as Freddy. He could smell the wind, and it wasn't blowing their way. So: he now knew who he had to screw, and was on course to do so.

He said to his secretary:

'Couple of calls, Bridget. Get me a chap called Maconochie. Lawyer in Perth. May be the name of the firm, may not. Then Andrew Meldrum at the Department of Resource and Development. Lunch, soon as he can. Savoy Grill.'

He didn't need to tell her to make sure the table she reserved was one of those against the wall. She knew his dislike of being exposed at a table in the middle of the restaurant.

'Perth, Australia or Perth, Scotland?'

When the police called her first reaction was anger.

'All right, then,' she said, 'it'll take me half an hour.'

'Be as quick as you can, Lady Leslie. It's a bit serious, I'm afraid.'

She knew Sergeant McGillycuddy, from the time when she had served on the children's panel, and she had always been struck by his good sense and decency. If he said it was serious, and didn't want to discuss it on the telephone, then there was cause for anxiety.

Bloody hell, she thought, bloody hell, he's been asking for it, the old fool, but bloody hell all the same.

She maintained her anger as she drove into the town. 'I wonder how much more I can stand,' she had said to Caro, as she set off, refusing Caro's offer to accompany her. It was a beautiful afternoon. The country was lush, still a score of shades of green. Cattle—Charolais solid and comforting as provincial France, Aberdeen-Angus gleaming sleep black—stood hock-deep in the fields by the river or vacant-eyed in the low water. Combines were already harvesting the first autumn-sown barley, and all the country spoke of warmth, fertility and goodness.

They were civil at the police station, even apologetic. Sergeant McGillycuddy brought her a cup of tea, which she didn't want.

'Aye,' he said, 'but this'll be a shock. You'll be better with the tea. I've put sugar in it, for the shock.'

She supposed he spoke from experience, and obeyed.

There had been a child, running out from behind an ice-cream van. Gavin had braked, but too late. The wing of the car caught the child and threw her across the road.

'Oh God,' she said.

'It could be worse. She might be dead. He might have killed her. We should be thankful he didn't. . .'

He had been breathalysed of course.

'It was a very high reading, Lady Leslie. I'm surprised he was in any sort of control with that high a reading.'

'Oh my God. How old was the girl? Is she going to be all right? Are you sure she's going to be all right?'

'Ten or eleven, I'm no sure. Aye, she's bruised and

shaken, but she's been very lucky. It's a mercy it wasn't worse. A very lucky wee girl.'

'Rosie's age,' she said. 'He might have killed her.'

'Aye, he might have. But she just dashed out from behind the van, you know. A sober driver would have been hard put to avoid her, a stone-cold sober one . . .'

'But he wasn't.'

'There's that. We've had to charge him of course. He's a bit shaken but the doctor's seen him.'

'It's hard to credit,' she said. 'What about her parents?'

'They've been notified. Well, in fact, the bairn's mother was at the scene of the accident, and the father's been notified. It'll maybe have taught the wee girl a lesson. And the mother. We ken the family fine. They're not folk that have a great care of their bairns. Irish. The father's been up for skelping them. I doubt he'll give the wee girl a few skelps the night.'

'I'll have to go and see them.'

'Well, that would be good of you, not that it'll do any good, you understand.'

'I wasn't thinking that way. And my husband, what about him?'

'Well, he's refused to see his lawyer.'

'I'm not surprised. He was seeing him about another matter this morning.'

'Is that so? It might be that that upset him. But now you're here, Lady Leslie, we can fix police bail.'

Sun, wine, and love had made them sleepy. Call the combination 'happiness' Kenneth thought, as he drifted off.

He woke, with Kat still asleep, her head resting on his shoulder, his arm cramped in the position from which he could not move it without waking her. What an odd thing flesh was: that one person's should delight and another's revolt. And love?

He had heard the opinion advanced that it was all an accident, a matter of propinquity at the right moment, of this and that; you could, the argument continued, fall in

love with anyone. To believe otherwise was Romantic nonsense, like pretending that love was for ever.

They had conducted that argument quite often. Rashid had laughed at him when he demurred.

'My dear Kenneth, nothing lasts, believe me, dear boy. When people stay together, it's only a matter of habit or convention, or fear. Love is desire, that's all, and you can't go on desiring the same fruit, old boy.'

That was so easy to say, so hard to disprove. What he felt for Kat felt as if it would last for ever. But that was like good weather. You couldn't believe it would ever end. And he had been in love before. But it hadn't been like this.

Pigeons cooed in the woods. He let his fingers play on her flat belly. They were lost in a world of green and sun and shadow.

Tony Lubbock enjoyed the surprise. He watched Susie flush. He saw evidence of guilt and anger at being found out flow into her face. He watched her hesitate between fear and indignation.

'You've not been so bloody faithful yourself,' she said.

'Did Eddie like him? Did you all have dinner together before you let him fuck you?'

'That's cheap. Like setting spies on your wife. I suppose it was that little runt Shane . . .'

'And if I've not been so bloody faithful, then at least I haven't done it in my own house . . .'

When they argued, they had developed the habit of never directly answering the other's accusation. They were well-matched, he had to concede that. He grinned at her, almost liking her for a moment, and feeling what he hadn't felt for a long time.

'You're a fine woman, Susie,' he said. 'Shame we've gone in different directions.'

'It's disgusting,' she said, 'the way you live. The way you are.'

Later, he heard her for a long time on the telephone. It wouldn't be Ted, she wouldn't be ready yet to play the

wounded daughter. It might be Debbie who was just the
sort of bitch to enjoy a heart-to-heart. It might be her lover.
He amused himself imagining that conversation. There
would be trouble there: Toby Crunning's wife was loaded,
and Toby prized his Lagonda, his yacht at Cowes, the
farmhouse in the Dordogne. Toby wouldn't be quick to
surrender all that. Toby would chicken out. Toby would
get on his knees to Maritsa and grovel. Pity he wouldn't be
able to watch him. But Susie was a fool if she thought Toby
would stick by her. You didn't change the habits of a
lifetime at forty-something. Not if you were a Toby.

The telephone clicked. What was she doing?

She was repairing her face. Of course she was. When
things went against Susie she retired to repair her face.

What he couldn't forgive her for was the way she had
brought up Eddie to despise and question the way he
himself lived. That wasn't right. He wouldn't forgive her
for that. She would repair her face but she wouldn't
come down to renew the battle. She would be scheming,
planning a way out which would leave her on top. He
knew her better than she knew herself.

The telephone rang. He answered it, hoping it would
be Toby Crunning. But it was a pinched, correct Scottish
voice, a voice he had grown up knowing and disliking.

'Mr Lubbock. This is Stuart Maconochie. I understand
you've been trying to get in touch with me. If you're who
I think you are, I'm honoured. What would a man like
you want from a humble country solicitor . . .?'

What is a humble country solicitor ready to give—or
sell? They fenced for a bit.

'But I understand, Mr Lubbock, you were in Perthshire
recently. Staying with Sir Gavin Leslie, am I right? Will
you have heard the bad news? Sir Gavin's had an
unfortunate accident?'

Has he now? Maconochie spilled the beans, one by
one. An understanding of sorts was reached.

Gavin came downstairs for drinks before dinner. His
hand trembled as he lifted the glass.

'Do you want to discuss this now or later?' he said.

'I don't see that there's anything to talk about,' Fiona said. 'There's nothing to talk about that we haven't talked about before, so there's nothing to talk about.'

XI

Every 14th July Mansie gave what he called 'A Reaction-ary and Feudal Party'. That was the way he saw himself now, though his father, the descendant of a line of tenant farmers in the Mearns, then Professor of Pastoral Theology at Edinburgh University, had been an exemplar of conventional bourgeois values, paying his bills, for instance, on the twenty-ninth day after receiving them. Mansie had been brought up in a flat in the New Town and educated as a day-boy at the Academy. No ghillie had applauded the young master's skill with rod or gun; summer holidays had been spent on the beach, golf-course and tennis-courts of Elie. But he had spent thirty years improving his past, and would (barring scandal) end his political career in the Lords.

In her early years of marriage, Fiona hated Mansie's parties. You never knew whom you would meet there. There had even once (before Mansie added the adjective 'Reactionary' to the description) been a member of the Rolling Stones. Or so she was told; she couldn't have identified any of them herself except the one with the thick lips. Now of course, she supposed, the Rolling Stones, about whom she had become more knowledgeable, would have qualified as reactionary and feudal themselves.

It was the element of surprise she hated then. She liked to know where she stood with people. She liked to know how they were going to behave. She liked social distinctions to be clear.

Recently she found herself looking forward to the parties. They were a change. When she now said to Kat, 'You never know who will be there,' she spoke almost with approval.

This year there was the bore of Gavin's disgrace. His shame hung over them. As she dressed she wondered if it was possible to disinfect herself.

Mansie rented one of the Straloch houses, Yallerlea, a Wagnerian fantasy built by the tenth Marquess, the father of the one Colonel Greenheart called 'the old Marquess'. That the tenth Marquess had had an heir was evidence of the power of the hereditary principle: he had been an aesthete later compelled by circumstance to abandon Yallerlea for the softer and more understanding charms of a villa on the Bay of Naples. His son had preferred the old family seat of Tullybrennan with its several ghosts who served, he discovered, as a delicious erotic stimulus to housemaids and debutantes. Yallerlea had stood uninhabited, but not empty, for many years till Mansie saw it as the perfect complement for his personality. Its last occupant had been the deserted wife of the tenth Marquess; her only alteration had been the conversion of a gallery (the paintings having already gone to Naples) into a Catholic chapel, where she had spent many hours recalling her husband's sins and (perhaps) pleading that they be forgiven.

'A perfect piece of late Victorian kitsch,' said Mansie, stroking his flowered silk waistcoat.

He liked to boast of the favourable terms of his lease.

'I have never shared my party's middle-class attachment to the idea of a property-owning democracy.'

Extravagantly illuminated, with the double doors that divided the two great saloons thrown open, with the statues of Ganymedes and nymphs bedecked with flowers, with its curious little anterooms, its three twisting staircases, its Alma-Tadema frieze, its velvet covered settees and its profusion of gilt, Yallerlea breathed an air of melancholy and faintly vicious dissipation.

'*Vesti la giubbia*', Mansie inscribed every year on his invitations.

*

110

'What does that mean?' Zoe asked Colin.

'On with the motley. The clown with his broken heart must still perform.'

'Is his heart broken?'

'No one has ever accused Mansie of having one. Appetites yes, heart no.'

'I don't get it.'

'And why should you?'

Fiona was amazed by Zoe. Mansie encouraged a certain extravagance of dress. Zoe had responded with zeal. She looked as if she was auditioning for *La Dame aux Camélias*, and expecting tough competition. It was Fiona's first sight of 'Colin's girl', and not one she was likely to forget.

Well, she would have to speak to her, was actually rather keen to do so, but before she could approach them, found Liz in front of her.

'You have to give it to Mansie,' Liz said. 'He may be the world's most godawful shit, but you have to hand it to him when it comes to parties. Lover-boy's eyes are on stalks. There'll be no holding him, I see. Everybody's here, Straloch himself, with a black girl, and . . . oh yes, Andrew. Did you know he was coming? Maybe he's staying with you . . .'

'Andrew? I'd no idea. What's brought him north, I wonder?'

'Sorry about old Gavin. Rotten luck.'

'Yes, rotten luck.'

'Brave of him to turn out . . .'

'Brave? Wild horses wouldn't . . .'

'I know Rory's dying to speak to him, tell him all about life inside. You remember Rory had his spell sewing mail-bags when that absolute stinker Sheriff Praitt said he was determined to make an example of him. Yonks ago, but Rory still wears the Old School Tie.'

'Yes, I remember.'

Reminiscences of the jug were one of Rory's party pieces.

*

Commiserations about Gavin's misfortune were the order of the first part of the evening. Fiona shrugged them off, unable to explain that she really didn't give a damn. But that was how she felt. She had gone to see the family of the injured girl. They hadn't been nice. She couldn't blame them for that. She wasn't sure that she could have been nice if it was the other way round. And then there was the class thing. They thought her condescending. Again, maybe she was. But she didn't see how else she could have done it. Anyway, she had done it. When she told Gavin, he looked at her as if she hadn't spoken and then turned away.

'You might have killed her,' she shouted after him. 'It might have been Rosie.'

He looked back at that, very slowly, as if he didn't see her, or anything else, and she couldn't read anything, not even misery, on his face.

And now Stuart Maconochie approached her:

'This is a bad business, Fiona,' he said, 'a very bad business. Of course Sir Gavin's been heading that way for a long time, and there are those who say he's just got what he's been asking for, but that doesn't alter the fact that it's a very bad business. And do you know, I'm a wee bit hurt. I gather Sir Gavin's employing Jim Thrussell of Thrussell & Thrussell. That's not right, you know . . .'

She hadn't expected to see Maconochie, which was absurd; he was Vice-Chairman of the Constituency Association.

'I don't know anything about that,' she said.

Colin and his extraordinary girl had vanished. Mansie encouraged his guests to roam everywhere.

'This is saturnalia,' he said, 'on with the motley.'

One year Liz had been discovered in the hay-bales with the Labour member for an Edinburgh constituency.

'Who would have thought Mansie would have had hay-bales in the stable?' she said.

This year Mansie had put the hired waiters into knee-

112

breeches. One year all the waiting had been done by girls from the local College of Further Education. That had been a mistake. By midnight not a waitress was to be found, not even the ugly ones. Now, as the band played the waltz from *Carousel* — Mansie had a thing about American musicals — she spotted Andrew eying the knee-breeches, or at least one pair of them.

'Sorry about Gavin, little Sis.'

'Oh bother Gavin. You should have let us know you were coming. We'd have put you up.'

'Sudden impulse. Leapt on the shuttle. Back south tomorrow. Don't suppose I need a bed . . .' he giggled '. . . not to sleep in.'

'You didn't travel dressed like that?'

'No, I changed here. This would look a bit OTT on a British Midland shuttle. Like it? I got it in Los Angeles at a sale of film gear at MGM. Mansie said, "Come as you see yourself". So I have. Mansie tells me old Colin's got a girl. What's she like?'

'An American half-wit, I gather.'

'Miaou, miaou, little Sis.'

'I wish you wouldn't call me that. Anyway it's not catty. I haven't actually met her. It's Liz who says she's a half-wit.'

'Old Liz. You won't believe this but I once went to bed with Liz.'

'Who hasn't?'

'Miaou, miaou again.'

'All right. I'm fond of Liz, but I still say, "who hasn't?" '

'You?'

'Don't be silly.'

'Fiona,' Andrew said. 'Tony Lubbock. Tell me about him.'

'Tony Lubbock?'

'Used to be a boy-friend of yours, didn't he?'

'That was ages ago. I haven't seen him in, well, not till a couple of weeks ago, why d'you want to . . ? I mean, what's Tony got to do with you?'

113

'That's what I want to know. What sort of chap is he? I barely met him when you and he . . .'

'What sort of chap?'

'Yes.'

But she couldn't answer, not honestly. It was the question she had been asking herself and none of the answers she had come up with were answers she could offer to Andrew. And then, looking at her brother's dark composed face, a face that had been schooled into carefulness and concealment of emotion, she read a twitch of anxiety there. He was afraid of Tony. That excited her, and then she was ashamed of her excitement. They had never been close, not after Andrew went to Prep School. They never conversed now, hadn't in ages. But he was flesh and blood, they had bathed in the same water as children, suffered alike at their mother's hands, both feared and resented her bullying.

'I wouldn't tangle with Tony,' she said.

'Thinks he's tough?'

'Is tough, I think . . .'

'Thanks, little Sis. I can be tough myself, in a feline way of course. Do something else for me, will you? Introduce me to Mrs Kemsley-Smith . . .'

'Enid? Why on earth? Oh, I see. Yes, well, you will be careful, won't you? Neighbours, you know.'

'I always am,' he said.

She knew he was lying, or at least lying to himself if he thought that.

'All right,' she said, 'we'll go look see. I think he's pretty ghastly myself . . .'

'But pretty. And sexy . . .'

Kenneth leant against a pillar and watched Kat dance with Mansie Niven. Mansie had been quick to annex her. 'It's my privilege as host to claim the right to dance with all the lovely girls, and this young lady is the tops.' Neither Kenneth nor Kat could object, but Kenneth watched Mansie closely all the same. It wasn't necessary; Kat wouldn't hesitate to smack a straying hand. She was astonishing, the way she adapted. This was all foreign to her, and yet . . . Kenneth saw her smile at Mansie, then she was laughing as Mansie swung her round, his monkey face lit up with excitement. Perhaps she was one to whom nothing was truly foreign, a girl so capable of accommodating experience that she would always be in control; everything on her own terms, because she saw the world only as it affected her. The thought surprised him. He hadn't ever considered her in that way before, and was disturbed. Yet he had always known she was a girl who knew where she was going, and knew she would get there. It was one of the things that kept them apart and yet drew him to her.

'*Odi vulgus profanum et arceo* . . .'

Colin lounged on a mock Louis Quinze settee in an ante-room, a cigar between his lips, and Zoe stretched on the Baluchi rug at his feet.

'Mansie's parties always inspire me to that sentiment.'

'You think they stink? Wha'does it mean?'

'I loathe and shun the vulgar throng . . .'

'Say, I like that.'

'Sikes doesn't care for Mansie or the vulgar throng.'

'Yeah, well I can see it would be a swell party if you liked swell parties.'

Colin took the cigar from his mouth and waved it like a conductor's baton. 'But I don't,' he said.

Zoe turned on herself like a serpent and laid her chin between Colin's knees.

'Aunt Ginny says this house gives her the most tremendous vibes. Isn't that just crazy?'

'Crazy.'

'Would you say I was crazy too if I told you you do something for me?'

'Yes.'

'Guess I'm crazy then.'

She crawled over him, wrapping her arms about his neck, then let her own head fall back and closed her eyes.

Colm McStay crooked a finger to summon Kenneth from

his pillar. He sat at a little table with a bottle of Jura whisky, three glasses, a packet of Capstan Full Strength and a pair of spectacles deployed before him. When Kenneth sat down he poured him a glass of whisky and pushed it across the table.

'What are you doing here?' Kenneth said. 'I thought Mansie banned journalists these days.'

'Och I'm here as an auld friend . . . no, better say, acquaintance, for Mansie has no friends. I was just thinking, how hard it is to recreate the decadence. Mansie works at it, but reality's too tough a competitor. You were looking lost, son, forlorn—there's a good archaic word for you.'

'Mansie's dancing with my girl.'

'Oh aye.'

'But I'll tell you what I was thinking also.' Kenneth hesitated over the offer. It wasn't the sort of thing he did, and he didn't really know Colm McStay and couldn't understand why he was impelled to confide in him.

'I was thinking that I'm more like Mansie than I am like Kat—that's my girl.'

'Well, I can see you are.'

'No, I'm not joking. It's just that I'm going to lose her.'

'Not to Mansie?'

'No. To the times we live in. Like Mansie they don't suit me.'

'Then make yourself fit them.'

Colm McStay lit a cigarette, poured himself more whisky and eyed Kenneth. Kenneth held his gaze a moment, then looked away. Kat and Mansie had vanished from the dance floor and from the room itself.

'If she's what you think she is, she'll fend off Mansie,' Colm McStay said. 'Laddie, I don't know why I'm taking the trouble because if I was to value you the way you value yourself, then the trouble would be wasted, and my breath too. And I don't know you well enough to know whether your estimate of yourself is right or not. But I liked your manners at that awful club of yours, and, as my old mother used to say, "a boy's judged by his manners, wherever he goes". She believed it, poor old besom. So I'll tell you this: there are things that aye outlast the times we live in, and the things that are most of the times go out of date. I'm in my middle fifties, you know, and I've seen things come and go. I've known them all, all the big politicians, from wee Attlee when I was but a laddie and Eden and Macmillan to the present lot. That's been my business. And I've spoken with every American president since Kennedy. They call me a reactionary, you know, and an anomaly—a Catholic Unionist who still thinks the British Empire was the greatest political creation since Ancient Rome, unless you consider the Holy Catholic Church as a political creation, which it is, thus bringing a contender into the ring . . .' He paused and sipped his whisky. 'Listen, laddie: this is no' just idle blethers. Do you know what Jack Kennedy once said to me? "None of this is worth doing, but it's a hell of a lot more worth doing than doing nothing . . ." I liked Jack, I couldn't thole Bobby, but I liked Jack. He was the right sort of Irishman: a pessimist filled with gaiety. And I don't mean a bloody queer like Andrew Meldrum.'

'Why're you telling me all this?'

'Drink up, laddie. For fortification, so that you can say: "there's nothing new and there's nothing true, and it don't signify"—that's old Thackeray by the way— "Nevertheless"—that's McStay. And if there's nothing true, then you've still got to act as if there was. . . .'

'Well,' Kenneth said, 'it's a logical inconsistency, isn't it? I mean if it was true that there was nothing true, that couldn't be true, could it? So it isn't.'

'You'll do, laddie. Now run along and take your girl off Mansie, and leave me to this Jura malt, which is not a bad malt, not at all a bad one. . .'

In the Turkish saloon, Ginny Prepper was holding court.

'The world's just crying out for Romance,' she said, 'and I sock it to them. I don't claim credit for my gift, it's just something that wells up in me. I believe in God and beauty and love and the spirit of place, and I just open my heart to experience and listen and obey its promptings. I guess it's a God-given gift, like having the sensibility that allows me to recall former existences. You-all have such past lives, but they're buried deep in most of you, and you can't lay hold of them. That's why Scotland means to me what it does . . . because I throb in response to its beauties and its horrors. I feel treachery at every corner because I experienced it, you see. It's the spirit speaking through me that my public responds to. They know I tell them what they need to hear and what the storm and stress of the world does not say to them.'

'She can go on like that for ever,' Zoe said.

'It's a rare gift indeed. Sikes of course has a clear memory also of past lives. And deaths.'

Kenneth roamed the house searching for Kat. A young man accosted him:

'I've seen you before. You're at Trinity aren't you? It was at one of Rashid's parties.'

Kenneth recognized the 'piece' at whom Andrew Meldrum had darted.

'Are you with Andrew?'

Rupert's mouth hung open. He put his hand on Kenneth's sleeve.

'That's rather the problem, you see. My parents are here, and I don't want them—Dad especially—to get the wrong idea.'

'You mean the right one, don't you?'

'Yes, I suppose I do. It is difficult, you see how it is . . .'

'Ah there you are at last, I've been looking everywhere for you.'

Andrew coming up behind Rupert, slipped his arm round his waist, and squeezed.

'I've been talking,' he said, 'to your charming mother. About Capri. I know it's old-fashioned, I said, but I adore Capri, and I've been lent this villa, and I'm sure Rupert would love it too. So would you, I said, why don't you both come and stay with me. Don't look like that, dearie, I'm an old campaigner, and I never forget that a boy's best friend is his mother. Not true in my case, I'm bound to say, but I'm sure in yours. . .'

When Andrew left her Fiona felt a need for fresh air. She slipped out into the night. There was a half-moon, the scent of roses and the air was warm. She crossed the dewy lawn to the terrace and leaned on the railing; honeysuckle twisted below her. It was a pity all the words used to describe the way things smelled were now tainted. She had no word for the perfume of the honeysuckle that didn't seem stale and cheap. But words, as she knew and had often regretted, did not come to her easily. She could be brisk and efficient in committee, but the words she used there were without resonance. Colin loved words, deployed them as defences; which was not how she wished she could use them. She would have liked to have the words which made her feelings ring true and the words were denied her. Perhaps that was because the feelings themselves were second-hand or stunted? This habit of introspection was new, a mark of discontent.

Andrew's mention of Tony Lubbock perturbed her. What was he up to? He couldn't be so naive as to suppose that he might somehow reach her through Andrew. So it must be something else. She tried to picture him, but the face slid away; and yet all at once, here, miles from him, in a garden he did not know, the ghost of a garden really, for Mansie had allowed it to run riot, she ached for him. If he had been there, she would have said, 'Take me'. Without hesitation. But without regret? That was another matter.

'What a mess.'

She spoke the words aloud, then looked round, anxious in case there was anyone to hear. But she was alone, in the darkness, in this spectral garden, which was dying even as it grew yearly more luxuriant.

Caro had said only the other day:

'If I had a place of my own, I would be a passionate

gardener. I see why it takes hold of people. It's ordered nature. A gardener's a sort of God making her own Eden.'

'With or without a serpent?'

'Oh Fi, we never get rid of the serpent.'

The Chinese parlour was always turned into a Men Only Bar at these parties. Women had been admitted in the early years, but the rise of feminism and more recently Political Correctness prompted Mansie to exclude them, according, as he said, to the principles of Reactionary Feudalism. He had even, despite his ban on journalists, troubled to telephone the gossip column of the most middle-class of the tabloids to register his decision. He had been rewarded with a photograph of himself goosing a chorus-girl.

'No contradiction,' says fun-loving MP. 'Everyone knows I adore women, but chaps must have a sanctum.'

However absurd the decree, many of his guests were duly grateful.

Conversation turned, as often that summer, to the question of the regiments.

'We've got half a dozen MPs here,' someone said. 'We ought to nail them to the cause.'

'What's the use?' Gavin pulled at his moustache. 'What's the bloody use of saving the regiment when we've got nothing left bloody well worth defending. Let it all go . . .'

Colonel Greenheart shook a weary head.

'You don't understand, Gavin. Speaking as a former military man, I must tell you that it's got damn all to do with the defence of the country . . .'

'Realm, you mean,' Rory said. 'Get it right, Gerry, for Christ's sake. Realm.'

'Damn all. The question is,' Gerry paused to collect his audience, 'the question is whether these shits in the Treasury and the Ministry of so-called Defence have the right to destroy the tradition of centuries and whether we are going to let them get away with it. A regiment's not just a fine fighting force or a fine body of men, it's a work of art. That's the point. What these shits are proposing is cultural vandalism.'

'With respect,' Stuart Maconochie leaned forward, adam's apple throbbing, 'with respect, Colonel, and speaking not as a lawyer or the constituency chairman, but as a man who has to make hard-headed decisions every day of the week, that's sentimental nonsense. The long and short of the bottom line is that it comes down to cost-effectiveness and the parameters of priorities, and when you consider the question in that light, then you have to find yourself in substantial agreement with the Treasury. No point, you know, in talking of a peace dividend, if nothing's paid out or invested as a result.'

'Maconochie,' Gavin said, 'why don't you just fuck off. I say, Fred, George whatever your name is . . .'

'Ambrose, sir.'

'Ambrose? You sure? All right, Ambrose, a spot more for everyone of whatever . . . Gerry? Rory?'

'Why not, old boy?'

'Why not?'

'Say not the struggle, as Colin would say . . . Where is the old thing?'

'Fucking around.'

'Really?' Colonel Greenheart watched Maconochie retire.

'That fellow,' he said, 'regular counter-jumper. Father was a decent stick, but son . . . NBG. RSW.'

'RSW?'

'Right wee shite, as Margot would say.'

'I've been looking for you everywhere.'

Caro laid her hand on Fiona's shoulder.

'Don't,' Fiona said. 'There's nothing wrong. Nothing new wrong. I like it here . . . There's something magic about gardens at night.'

'Dangerous magic . . .'

'All magic's that, surely . . .'

The girls leaned over the railing. Fiona moved her arm

121

a little so that their elbows were no longer touching. They didn't speak. Fiona knew that speech would lead them into undergrowth which she preferred to leave unexplored. She sensed that Caro was longing to guide her there, dared not make the move. Yet there was no sense of strain. It was as if alternative futures were held in suspense, like Mushtaq and Kirstie, the Dandie Dinmont, sharing the hearth rug before a roaring fire, dozy in the happy heat, yet wary of each other. But of course Caro might not be thinking of that at all. You could never tell even when you were certain you knew.

'You know,' she said, 'as I get older, I become more and more aware of the otherness of other people.'

'Is that a warning?'

'No,' Fiona said, 'it's an expression of puzzlement.'

'Well,' Caro said, 'Colin getting off with that half-wit is certainly evidence that you never know other people. I saw them going up towards the bedrooms as I came out.'

'Oh you must have heard Colin talk of "young friskers".'

'I've heard him talk. I didn't think it went further than talk.'

'There you are then.'

'Fi . . .'

She laid her hand on Fiona's arm. Again Fiona shook it off.

'Don't you see,' she said, 'there's no point. I can't stop thinking about Tony . . .'

Caro let her hand drop.

'Well,' she said, 'I don't know what to say. What was that?'

'It sounded like a scream.'

'Fun and games. Or a peacock.'

'Aren't any peacocks here, except Mansie. There it is again. It's from somewhere down on the terrace.'

They pushed their way through the fringes of rhododendrons which had encroached on the path that led to the lower terrace. The sound of a girl's voice came to them, and they quickened their pace stumbling over roots. Fiona nearly fell once, and lost one of her shoes on the descent. So she kicked off the other. It was darker on the lower terrace and the lights of the house looked far away and gave no illumination there. But sounds of a struggle guided them, and Caro called out, and then there was silence.

'Who's there? What's happening?'

A figure lurched out of the bushes, stumbling against Fiona, putting the shoulder in, and depositing her in a bush. It did not pause, but took off in the direction of the house.

'Extraordinary.'

There was a sound of sobbing. Caro pushed forward. It was too dark to see anything. She called out again.

'Who are you? Come here. It's all right.'

Fiona struggled out of the bush.

'He's gone. It's all right.'

They huddled together in a bedroom. Kat was white-faced and trembling. She held the glass of brandy in both hands. Fiona and Caro waited for her to speak.

'Don't if you don't want to,' Fiona said, longing for her to do so. 'You might feel better.'

'You fought him off,' Caro said. 'Didn't you?'

The man who knocked her into the bush had been smaller and heavier than Kenneth, Fiona was sure of that. Anyway, Kenneth wouldn't, would he? And he wouldn't have had to either. There was that.

'He tried to rape me, he bloody tried to rape me . . .'

'Has he a name?' Caro said.

'I saw you with Mansie, was it Mansie?' Fiona said.

Kat nodded. She was crying and still shaking.

'He bloody tried.'

Liz stopped Kenneth on a staircase.

'That woman's mad,' she said, 'clinical. I suppose it's refreshing in small doses. She has just told Rory that she is sure he was Bothwell in a previous life. Crazy. Rory didn't know where to look.'

'Well, she thinks Rupert Kemsley-Smith used to be Lord Darnley. I think he rather fancies the notion.'

'Meanwhile, have you seen lover-boy?'

''Fraid not. Have you seen Kat? The girl I came with?'

'No.'

Liz sighed.

'These Australians,' she said. 'I don't trust lover-boy an inch. I wouldn't trust him not to get off with the Queen's Corgis.'

'It's a matter for the police. I'm going to call them.'

But though Caro spoke as if she was certain, she didn't move. Instead she looked at Fiona, who, conscious of the scrutiny, kept her eyes down, examining her fingernails. Why had Kenneth let Kat go off with Mansie, and why indeed had she agreed to go into the garden with him? But that was silly. She had gone into many gardens herself, with different men, without being raped, with Mansie himself if it came to that.

'We can't let him get away with it,' Caro said.

Yes, well, she knew the argument, and in general she agreed with it. She would never have called herself a feminist, but that didn't mean she wouldn't stand up for her sex. Only . . . part of the trouble was of course that she had never been able to take Mansie seriously, even though she knew of occasions when he had acted with decision and to effect.

Still Kat said nothing. She looked like a schoolgirl. She had lost all the assurance that had impressed Fiona.

There was no one they could consult. This was a matter they had to decide between the three of them.

'Kat?' she said. 'What do you think?'

The girl shook her head.

What surprised Fiona was that Mansie had run away. She would have expected him to brazen it out.

'I don't care,' Caro said. 'He shouldn't be allowed to get away with this.'

'Don't, Caro,' Fiona said. 'There are other considerations.'

There always were. That was something she had learned. And as usual some of them were shaming, which didn't mean that you didn't have to give weight to them. There was, first, obviously, the political element. Fiona didn't these days have much time for that sort of thing. Any beliefs had long withered. In certain moods she found herself, to her surprise, agreeing with Colin's view of these matters: that they were risible. Nevertheless she couldn't be entirely indifferent, and she knew others would be even less so. Mansie was their MP, and a Tory and a Unionist, and this would be a really lovely scandal for the Socialists and the Nats. Few of her friends would thank her if she gave them that sort of meal.

Then there was Kenneth. This girl was good for him. How would his relationship be affected? It was foolish to pretend that that didn't matter. Surely Caro must see that too.

And there was the girl herself. How did she feel about it? Would she really be ready for the questioning and the medical examination and a court appearance? And what about her parents? Fiona knew little of them, only what Kenneth had said in that vague manner of his.

Damn. Damn Mansie.

There were fewer people on the dance floor now. The party had broken up into cabals and couples. Kenneth, searching for Kat and sorry for himself, came upon Andrew Meldrum looking his age as he now too often did towards midnight.

'That little bitch,' Andrew said, 'has gone off with that slut from Oz. If she thinks I'm taking her to Capri after this, she's got another think coming.'

'Do you mean Rupert?' Kenneth said. 'He's with the American woman being questioned about his past life.'

'Well, that is something I should like to hear.'

'She thinks he used to be Lord Darnley.'

'Does she? I see the resemblance, of course.'

In the Men Only Bar, Colonel Greenheart said:

'I don't know just what the monkey's doing, but it's a very remarkable painting.'

'Dirt, pure dirt. Jolly enough, mind you,' said Arthur.

'How much?'

'Young Straloch is thinking of buying it back. He says it belongs in Tullybrennan. I'm not so sure myself.'

'It's rather Mansie's kind of thing from the sound of it.'

'So she's gone and left you.'

Colm McStay pushed the bottle towards Kenneth.

'Take a sup, laddie.'

His red-mottled face shone with good-humoured malice. He was, as he often said, a connoisseur of broken passions. Congenital Puritanism had destroyed his own marriage as much as selfishness, booze, and infidelity. He had a reputation which made women fall easily in love with him; he treated them all with contempt. He understood why, and was amused by the reason: 'I could never marry a woman who didn't measure up to my old mother,' he would say, 'and all those I fancy are her opposite.' Then he smiled, and drank some more whisky, and watched the effect this had on women. Now he said to Kenneth:

'So she's given you the slip? Eh, laddie? You're out of date. I can read you like a *Sun* editorial. You still believe in Romance, with the twentieth century all but shot its bolt, in true Hollywood romance, and you haven't learned that women don't give a damn now.'

Kenneth poured himself a glass, and sat, holding it but not drinking, while Colm McStay talked of his own first love, from a Glasgow suburb, when they were both young at the Uni, in the days when Glasgow was still a black manufacturing city, but the grass was green and the flowers bloomed in Kelvin Park. As he spoke, the old journalist's eye grew liquid and the glottal stop was more apparent. But all the time he was watching Kenneth. It was a performance he had given often, and meant nothing. 'Will I speak of Kat sometime in this way?' Kenneth thought.

Then Colm McStay said:

'You won't believe it, laddie, but Mansie was a Romantic too once. And now he's come to this play-acting. We all come to play-acting and he's maybe more honest. We come to play-acting, aye, you're right. I'm a comedian myself, because you see the intelligent man can't go on buying what life sells him.'

He picked up the whisky bottle and stroked it, and laid it against his cheek.

'Here's comfort,' he said, 'for the cheat life plays on us. For its false prospectus. If it wasn't that, then getting fou would be nothing but greed. And, by the cardinal's braces, it is greed.'

Through the cigarette smoke Kenneth looked at a huge, bad fake-Classical painting: the Baths of, he thought, Caracalla, thronged with curly-headed ephebes in languorous attitudes, the Tenth Marquess's taste, also Andrew Meldrum's if it came to that.

Colm McStay followed his gaze.

'Reminds me of a note in one of Corvo's letters,' he said. 'Terrible, isn't it. There was a painter called Tuke—fisher-boys in Cornwall, that sort of thing. Corvo or Rolfe, whichever you prefer, had tried to lure him to Venice with a promise of delights available. Tuke wouldn't budge. And Rolfe said testily: "It's absurd of Tuke to say he can get all he wants in Falmouth." '

'The one on the extreme left,' Kenneth said, 'is rather like young Rupert, don't you think?'

'It's an awful painting.'

'Awful.'

'But then it's an awful house. Suits Mansie of course.'

Fiona said:

'Caro, I'm going to find Kenneth. Then you and he can take Kat home. Then I'll speak to Mansie.'

'Not Kenneth,' Kat said. 'Take me home, but I couldn't face Kenneth yet. I feel dirty. And no police, no police please.'

'All right,' Fiona said. 'But I think I should tell Kenneth.'

'No, not now, please, not ever.'

'All right. That can wait. Maybe you'd prefer to tell him yourself.'

'I don't believe it,' Kat said. 'I just don't believe it. It happened to me but I don't believe it. Do you know what he said? "I'll show you where the white lilies grow, on the banks of Italy." It doesn't make sense, but I can't get it out of my head.'

'I wouldn't worry. We all know Mansie's cracked.'

Fiona wasn't imaginative. She recognized this as a deficiency in herself, though it was one that hadn't troubled her, and indeed, for a long time, she would remark on it with a certain self-satisfaction. Yet as she moved through the crumbling party in search of Mansie, Kat's incredulity impressed her. None of this was real. Even the naughtiness wasn't real. The decadence in which the Tenth Marquess had indulged had been just that: self-indulgence. It suited Mansie of course, because, even if it wasn't exactly true that he was cracked, he was a person you couldn't take seriously. But then which of them was? Not Gavin, certainly. And what did it mean to be a person you took seriously? There were the children of course . . . Charlie and Rosie were serious. Everything that happened mattered to them. But for how long?

She saw Kenneth through a doorway talking to a middle-aged red-faced man with thin stubbly grey hair. Kenneth was sideways on to her, and his head was angled so that his rather long hair obscured his face. Two hundred years ago, he would have called Mansie out: swords or pistols at dawn. Now, the terrible thing was he wouldn't do anything but be hurt. Tony would screw Mansie, but Kenneth would just keep his distance, and make jokes about him. Like Colin. How tired she was of jokes. Of course it had always been agreed that she had no sense of humour. That wasn't such a bad thing, when having a sense of humour meant that nothing mattered.

On the staircase she encountered Liz.

'I'm bereft,' Liz said, waving a champagne glass and spilling some of the wine. 'Rory's vanished with that American loony, and lover-boy . . . well, lover-boy meets lover-boy. Story of my life.'

'Poor Liz.'

'Well, at least he needn't trot out that story of why he left his dance company in Australia to me again.'

'Have you seen Mansie?'

'Poor Fiona. It hasn't come to that.'

'Not exactly.'

'Well, that's something. No, I haven't. Incidentally Gavin is lying dead drunk on a sofa on the second landing. But I don't suppose that worries you.'

'Not at all . . . I've given up on Gavin, you know.'

'Can't say as I blame you. Balls to them all, I say.'

Gavin lay with his mouth open, face red and puffy, bow-tie dangling and collar loose. He gave a single snore and turned over, away from her, burying his face in a cushion. It was the way Charlie turned over in bed, but the resemblance brought no feelings of tenderness. It rather intensified her exasperation. He was cheating Charlie as he had cheated her.

She found Mansie in a little room off the library. He was with a young dark-haired girl whom she didn't recognize. He had his arm round her shoulder and their faces were close together, and he was speaking in a low voice little more than a whisper. He looked at Fiona with irritation, and made a gesture with his free arm inviting her to leave.

But instead she advanced into the room and approached the sofa and stood over them. The girl looked up, embarrassed.

'Do you mind leaving? I must speak to Mansie.'

The girl hesitated.

'Please,' Fiona said.

'All right,' Mansie said, 'five minutes. Don't run away, child.'

Fiona watched the girl out of the room. At the door she looked over her shoulder and smiled to Mansie, gave a little wave, and closed the door behind her.

'This is monstrous, Fiona, I was just getting acquainted with that charming filly.'

'Oh yes. Quick work. You really are a bastard, Mansie. Do you realize what you've been up to tonight? If Kat wasn't a nice girl, and shy, it would be a matter for the police.'

'I don't know what you're talking about.'

Mansie took a jewelled snuff-box from his fob pocket, extracted a pinch of snuff, placed it in the hollow made on the back of his other hand by extending his thumb, and sniffed deeply.

'You tried to rape her. That's what I'm talking about.'

'Oh balls and poppycock, a little scuffle in the bushes, that's all. Really, it's too bad. She's been reading too many magazine articles, that little girl. What a baby! I found her charming and absolutely acquiescent, and then she suddenly said, "no", so I desisted, rather annoyed I may say because she had wasted valuable time. I'm the one with cause to complain.'

'You really are a bastard, Mansie.'

'Not at all. Nothing happened. Call it the influence of the moon. Say I was carried away. Say I'm sorry if you like. But really, I must say, I go to enormous trouble and expense to lay on the sort of party which, though I say it myself, that little suburban miss has never seen the like of and then this is my reward. Really, people are so ungrateful. I must say I had thought better of you, Fiona. I've always thought you a sensible girl.'

'Oh yes,' she said, 'I am sensible. So's Kat. That's why the police haven't been called in. But this is a warning, Mansie. Another time, and I'll be sensible in a different way. And what about Kenneth?'

'Kenneth? What about him?'

'She's his girl.'

'Oh that sort of proprietorial attitude's out of date. Are you faithful to Gavin, my dear?'

XII

Clouds hung over the hills behind which the sun had already slid. Seagulls squawked as the haar crept in on the land. Fiona sat on the damp rocks, her Barbour pulled around her, while Solomon lay at her feet and Kirstie hunted rabbits among the whins. It was one of those evenings in the first weeks of August when autumn has already come to Scotland. She could smell the sea though it was more than a mile off. Cattle were dark uncertain shapes in the fields on the other side of the river which Tony was fishing.

She was happy for the moment because she was alone and he was engaged in an activity which demanded all his attention and which made him happy. But he would stride up the bank and they would retire to the hotel and he would make demands over dinner which she couldn't satisfy. That was why she had brought the dogs: as a species of bulwark.

'Well,' he said, 'at least they're not your children.'

But that was a mistake. He realized that almost before the words were out, and began to talk of other matters, praising her looks, not understanding that this praise wasn't what she wanted. That wasn't his fault. He couldn't know what she wanted, since she didn't herself.

There was no sound but the gulls and the surge of water, and Kirstie in the whins. She fondled the velvet of Solomon's ear, which was cold to the touch. What had she replied? That the children were staying with friends which was why she had been able to accept his invitation, delivered just like that, with a casualness that made it sound half a command, half a whim. And he had been

131

good so far. He had devoted himself to his fishing. She might have been bored out of her mind and it wouldn't have mattered to him.

He had booked a separate room for her in the little fishing hotel.

'They know me here,' he had said. 'They do you well.'

That was a lie, surely, that they knew him. Hadn't he said that he hadn't been in Scotland for years, that time when they met in Edinburgh? But then it turned out not to be a lie. The proprietor had recently moved there from the south, and he did indeed know Tony, and spoke as if they were old friends.

Giving her this time by herself, near him but yet alone, might be what he thought of as good tactics.

The light was fading fast.

Over their meal, while there were other people in the little dining-room, where the curtains were drawn and a log fire burned, he talked of this and that, nothing to disturb. He did it easily, not as if it was an effort to make conversation, and his confidence rendered her more nervous. They ate a steak from the salmon he had caught the day before, with gooseberry sauce and new potatoes, and drank a bottle of real Chablis. She was surprised to find herself hungry.

'Were you surprised I asked you here?'

They were alone, over coffee and brandy for Tony. She had declined a liqueur. He clipped the end off a cigar and lit it.

'Makes me happy,' he said. 'When you said "yes", I could hardly believe it, though of course deep down I've never doubted that . . . '

'Stop it, Tony,' she said. 'I don't know why I've come. It was madness.'

He laid his hand on hers.

'Don't worry,' he said, 'I'm not going to rush things.'

He began to speak about his own marriage. It had always been second-best, he said.

'It was a long time before I admitted that to myself.

There was a lot of pride involved. Now it's over. Whatever you decide it's over. We're through,' he said, 'Susie and me. I've moved out, been staying in a flat the firm has in the Barbican. Won't ask you there. You'd hate it. But don't worry,' he said again. 'I'm not trying to rush you. You have all the time you want.'

She wished she could have replied with a happy marriage. But she thought of Gavin as he had been since the accident, and if she was honest, since long before it, but so much worse since; for a moment she was afraid she was going to cry.

'Do you have children?' she said. 'I don't know anything about you really.'

'One boy.'

She waited for him to go on, but he leaned back in his chair, taking his hand off hers, and drew on his cigar.

'You know,' he said, 'with Susie it was just sex. And the need to be married, and pride of possession. Like owning an Aston Martin. Possessions mattered to me then.'

'Don't they now?'

He smiled as if acknowledging the irony in her voice.

'No,' he said. 'Success matters. Making things happen. But possessions as such, no, not now . . . Susie's brought my son up to despise me.'

'That's terrible,' she said, and meant it. She would always work to keep Charlie from despising Gavin. 'But for what? You don't seem so despicable to me.'

'She's turned into a *Guardian* woman,' he said. 'I don't stop to think if I'm unhappy, but I suppose I've been unhappy in my marriage for a long time. I can tell you that. I wouldn't say it to anyone else.'

'And what about her?' she said. 'Is she unhappy?'

'Oh yes,' he said.

Silence fell between them. She sensed that he was content with the silence, which wasn't a silence of distance. Yet the intimacy he had established was disturbing in its way, inviting her to accept the premises of his argument.

'Your husband's in a mess,' he said. 'I know that. I've been in touch with his lawyer. I'm prepared to help, buy the land he's going to have to sell. Maconochie's ready to cheat him. I can see to it that he doesn't.'

'Is this another way of trying to buy me?'

'Yes,' he said, 'of course it is. You won't leave him while you feel guilty towards him. I know that.'

He was right of course.

'How can you know that?' she said. 'You hadn't thought of me for years till this summer . . .'

'Oh yes, I had . . . I've been having business dealings with your brother Andrew also.'

He sat back smoking and watching her. She dropped her eyes.

'Don't trust him,' she said.

'Oh,' he said, 'it's not a question of that. I'll have to apply a little pressure. It won't be difficult.'

'Andrew's tough, you know. Tougher than he looks.'

'But vulnerable. As a politician.'

He pushed his chair back and got to his feet. He walked over to the window, drew back the curtain. Smoke drifted over his shoulder. His hair was growing grey and he didn't stand quite straight.

'It's stopped raining. Your dogs will need a walk.'

They followed the path along the river that led to the sea. There was no wind. Yet the breath of the sea seemed to bring chill movement to the mist that enclosed them. For the first part of the walk the way was so narrow that they were compelled to go one behind the other, Solomon brushing Fiona's heels while Kirstie darted in and out of the whins. Duck rose from the water's edge with an angry squawk and a rapid beating of wings. They smelled the sea and then heard the waves as the path broadened and they were able to walk side by side.

'My father never saw the sea till he was forty,' Tony said.

He began to talk about his family and the Ukraine. He had never done so in their youth when he had been concerned to fit in, to conceal whatever was different about him. She had never questioned his background then; perhaps he had been ashamed of his parents. Now he spoke differently, with pride and affection.

'They were casualties,' he said, 'though they recovered. It's because of my father's experience that I have no time for politics. He used to tell me that his brother was an idealist. This brother was ten years older, or something like that, and one of those who believed in the Revolution. That cut him off from the family, according to my Dad. They thought he was a traitor. Dad gave the impression that they were big landowners. That may have been on his mother's side, I don't know. Dad used to say he was a lawyer, but so many of them said that. Doesn't matter, but this uncle disappeared into the *gulag* or was killed in one of Stalin's purges, I don't know which. That's why I've never been able to believe in politics in this country. In our experience politics is a matter of life and death, and I hate the whole thing. Does that make sense to you? I can't take someone like your brother Andrew seriously.'

'No one's ever taken Andrew seriously, except himself,' she said.

'You know what I want, Fiona,' he said. 'I want to marry you.'

'But it's crazy,' she said, 'we don't even know each other.'

Still he didn't touch her. She knew that if he did it would determine things one way or the other, but she couldn't know which way till it happened. Maybe he was afraid.

'There's all sort of reasons why it's crazy,' she said. 'I don't think I could share your life.'

'You're unhappy,' he said. 'You're unhappy with your own.'

'That's not the point.'

She turned away from him and walked towards the sea. Kirstie gambolled around her, charging into the waves and biting them. Fiona held out her finger to the spray rebounding from a rock, and licked it. The taste of salt water on skin was good. A big wave surged against her, reaching almost the tops of her wellingtons. There was no sound but the sea and Tony waiting. She could hear him waiting.

'That's not the point,' she said again, but it was no good; he wouldn't believe that. His self-control only made the wildness of his obsession clearer to her. He was waiting because he was confident of victory.

'That's not the point.'

'You're working hard to convince yourself,' he said, 'but what other point is there?'

'You thought I was afraid when we broke up years ago.'

'Yes.'

'What makes you think I'm not afraid now?'

'It's not fear that's holding you back this time,' he said.

I don't know, she thought. If it was fear it would all be easy. I might despise myself, but what's new in that, and it would still be easy. And it wasn't only fear that I felt before. There was distaste too. Only I can't tell him that. But there was distaste, and it hasn't all gone.

'I've made too many mistakes,' she said.

Still he held off, and that made her nervous. It was like being ground down by his will. But she had a native obstinacy that resisted. It was what had seen her through before now. It was what marked her out, she had often thought, from the rest of the family: this determination to be ruled by what she saw as duty. She never spoke of this because it made her seem priggish, and she knew that she was priggish and didn't like it: the Head Girl again. But she had a text or motto which she kept close to her heart: 'There are no Rights and plenty Duties'. She had no duty towards Tony.

Again she licked the salt water from her fingers.

'I had an affair once,' she said. 'I loathed it.'

'I'm not suggesting an affair,' he said. 'I don't want an affair. If that was all you offered me, I would walk away from it.'

'It's no good,' she said. 'Can't you see that? There's too much stacked against it.'

'You're not happy. When I saw you in the NB I knew you weren't happy.'

'Oh happy,' she said, 'could you make me happy? What makes you think you could make me happy? And do you believe in happiness yourself? Is that what's important to you?'

'It's what I need,' he said. 'It's what's been missing in my life too.'

She shook her head. Solomon pushed his nose against her legs. She leaned down and scratched him behind the ear. There was a point of light out to sea, a fishing-boat , she supposed.

Maybe I'll take a rod tomorrow, she thought, or maybe I'll go home before breakfast. Well, after breakfast. It's not going to work. I didn't know when I came how it might work. I only came because nothing else was working. But this can't work either. We're as distant from each other as that fishing-boat is from the shore.

'You'd be bored with me,' she said, 'almost as soon as you'd got what you think you want.'

'No,' he said, 'no.'

He picked something up and threw it out to sea. Solomon launched himself in pursuit, swimming heavily towards an invisible and unattainable target. It was a long time before he gave up. Negatives hung damp and chill as the encircling mist.

XIII

There came a week of wet days, rain driven on a cold wind from the north-west. Kenneth sat by the library fire reading Sir Walter Scott. He worked his way through *Waverley*, *Guy Mannering* and *The Antiquary*. It was easy to picture himself in the role of the colourless heroes. If he wrote a novel it would have such a figure at the centre. One evening at Cambridge a friend had urged him to read Lermontov: *A Hero of our Time* spoke to him directly. The concept of 'the superfluous man', unable to settle in the time and situation in which he finds himself, unable to discover anything of urgency, unable to believe in the ideas of the day, appealed to him. Scott's heroes were of the same order, whether Sir Walter recognized it or not.

No letter came from Kat. Kenneth wrote to her twice that week, found the words he wanted to write evading him. 'The sweet language of love', which had come so naturally to the nineteenth century, rang like counterfeit coin.

Things between them had changed after Mansie's party. He didn't know why.

The mood of the house oppressed him. It reflected his own lack of purpose. Even Fiona was distant when they met which was only at meals. He was accustomed to thinking of her as positive. Now she and Caro sniped at each other, but when he questioned his sister, she denied any quarrel.

'I'm beginning to think I made a mistake in coming home from New York,' she said.

As for Gavin, his state appeared hopeless. He lurked in his business-room, not even coming to table. That was a relief. When Fiona looked at her husband, Kenneth read hatred in her eyes.

He settled in his chair by the fire, a spaniel at his feet, and opened *The Heart of Midlothian*. 'The times have changed in nothing more,' he read, 'than in the rapid conveyance of intelligence and communication betwixt one part of Scotland and another.'

'Not here,' he said to the spaniel. 'You dogs communicate. Nobody else does much.'

He gave the dog a slice of the anchovy toast he had brought from the kitchen, and ate another piece himself. He looked out at the pools of water on the lawn, the tattered roses, the dark gloom of dripping rhododendrons.

Caro found Fiona mucking out the stable. The work brought some colour into her cheeks, for the first time, Caro thought, since she had returned from her week-end (which hadn't actually been a week-end, but that was how she thought of it) with Tony Lubbock.

'He telephoned,' she said, 'but rang off when it was me that answered. Is he afraid of me?'

Fiona didn't answer, but dug the fork under a clod of dung and wet straw.

'I can't think why you have to bring them in at night,' Caro said. 'Surely they can be out at grass.'

'All this rain, wet grass, Laminitis.'

'I suppose you know best.'

She leaned against the wall and watched her. Fiona worked carefully, filling the barrow in layers. Sounds of activity came from the straw-shed beyond, where the Dandie Dinmont was ratting.

'What have I done wrong?' Caro said. 'You can't blame me for disapproving.'

Fiona withdrew the barrow from the box, and moving backwards pulled it out of the stable, turning it in the yard and heading for the midden. Caro waited her return. After a few minutes Fiona came back, the barrow empty and a lock of damp hair lying over her cheek.

'You can't mean to go off with him,' Caro said.

Fiona pushed the barrow into the adjoining box and resumed work. There was a hollow in the floor where cobbles had worked themselves loose and been removed, and when she lifted the drenched straw from it, there was a stench of ammonia.

'I had a word with Andrew about Master Lubbock,' Caro said. 'There's some deal that's got stuck and he's been putting pressure on Andrew. Andrew said "pressure", that was his word, but it sounds like blackmail to me. There's something fishy about his company, Andrew says. He thinks the Fraud Squad are interested. The Serious Fraud Squad, I think it's called.'

Fiona gave no sign that she had heard, but continued to work.

'Andrew says he's a crook, whatever the Fraud Squad decides, and a bully.'

She started to cry. Fiona still paid no attention. When she had cleared the box, she pulled the barrow out of the stable, and then began to scatter straw. Then she filled the three haynets, and took the buckets away, and filled them at the tap in the yard and replaced them. Through her tears Caro saw the slim figure in jeans and a torn jersey working as if she wasn't there.

'You've made up your mind, haven't you,' she whimpered. 'You're going to have him, aren't you.'

Satisfied that the stable was ready for occupation, Fiona took the barrow down to the midden to empty it. When she returned she swept up the loose straw and any dung that had fallen off the barrow with a broom. Then she whistled to Kirstie and returned towards the house, leaving Caro still in tears.

Silence was a weapon, silence was a defence. Fiona had learned that early. It had been for years her only method of dealing with her mother. She retreated into silence whenever she was hurt, or uncertain or angry. And she was all these things now. She recognized that she was being unfair to Caro whose only offence was that she had

140

declared love for her and attempted to invade areas of life which Fiona preferred to shut off from the world. As she made her way back to the house, she envied Kenneth who lost himself in novels, or Colin who protected himself with gin. Perhaps even Gavin, though she couldn't believe that he was now finding liquor any valuable defence against reality.

It was too early to bring the horses in, too early by hours, and she couldn't stand the confinement of the house with the ever present chance that Tony would call again. She turned away, heading for the woods by the loch, with Kirstie delighted at the prospect of switching attention to the possibility of rabbits.

Caro didn't understand why she avoided Gavin, and why she could not bring herself to speak to him when they did encounter. She didn't realize that Fiona couldn't trust herself to stop at speech if she once allowed herself to address him.

She welcomed the rain and the chill wind on her face, the sharp scent of the pines and the grey light. When she reached the boathouse she sat under the cover of the verandah roof and watched the rain spit on the black water. She composed letters in her head to Tony, and knew that they were letters she could never send.

Colin sat in the bar of the Graham Arms drinking gin with Zoe. Sikes lay at their feet chewing a table-leg.

'Can't you stop him, Colin?' Mr Smith said. 'I'll have no bloody furniture left.'

'No,' Colin said, 'not unless you have a bone.'

'I'll see what I can find. Bloody dog.'

Zoe said, 'of course I've always known she was off the wall, but now she's as crazy as a coon. It's this Mary, Queen of Scots thing. You tell me, Colin, why anyone should want to think she was her? Sounds like she was a loser to me, and whatever you say of Aunty Ginny, she's not that. And she's crazy about Rupert though anyone can see he's as gay as San Francisco.'

'Queer as Dick's hatband,' Colin said.

'Now she wants Liz to put on a Tableau Vivant at her festival with her as Mary.'

'At Fotheringay, I trust.'

'Come again.'

'That's where she was beheaded.'

'I guess that might draw the crowds, but no such luck. Honestly, I've been accustomed to thinking I'm not all there myself, but compared to her, well . . .'

'The bits of you that are there are very nice.'

Mr Smith returned with a manky-looking bone. Sikes deigned to investigate it, then resumed work on the table-leg.

'Sikes prefers a challenge,' Colin said.

'Sure does.'

'Will you marry me?'

'Marry you?'

'That's right. With this ring I thee wed.'

'You're crazy. You know that, you're crazy.'

'If you like,' Colin said, 'nevertheless . . .'

'Have you been married before?'

'Certainly have.'

'And now you want to marry me?'

'Certainly do.'

'You're crazy.'

Zoe thrust a finger under the hem of her cycling shorts and scratched her thigh.

'Don't see why not though,' she said.

They had almost stopped taking meals together. Food was placed on the sideboard, and each entered separately, took what they wanted and retired to a part of the house where they hoped to be undisturbed: Gavin to his study (where the food would mostly remain uneaten); Fiona to the little sitting-room where she had talked to Tony Lubbock, and Kenneth to the library. Only Caro settled herself at the dining-table and ate there. Tonight, however, she found herself unable to eat. She stood by the window. Rooks and jackdaws hurled themselves across the sky. A wind was rising.

There was a thin slice of new moon. Little branches of a climbing rose beat feebly on the window-pane. She was very conscious of the silent breathing throughout the house; it seemed that nothing could exist beyond it. She had to leave, return to New York, start again in London; and yet she couldn't bring herself to shift.

A car drew up braking too fast scattering the gravel. Enid Kemsley-Smith and Ginny Prepper emerged. Caro slipped behind the curtain, and listened to the silence that followed the ringing of the bell. Then she heard footsteps on the gravel. She saw Enid peer into the dining-room, heard her say:

'Strange. Can't believe they're all out.'

Heard the jackdaws call, footsteps retreating, car doors slamming and engine start. Felt the silence return to close around the house.

XIV

Tony Lubbock knew himself to be stranger than he let on. He had spent quarter of a century passing himself off as a regular guy, one of the boys, on the way up, but with absolutely conventional tastes. Freddy, who thought he knew him better than anyone, had accepted him as just that. And most of the time Tony allowed himself to think he was no more than that. But there was that compartment where the memory of Fiona was locked up; there was, too, a deep-rooted irony which wasn't the comfortable English variety that is only understatement, an irony that can co-exist happily with the knowledge that the English are a Chosen Race and that all is ultimately for the best in the best of all possible Home Counties. Tony knew that nothing was for the best, that permanence was illusory, that predators prowled round the stockade. It was his irony that gave him his contempt for the law, that made him respect conventions only while they suited him. Sometimes, at a business meeting or while smoking a cigar after a good dinner, he seemed to stand outside himself, to be able to look at his life as if it was a comedy being played in a proscenium arch theatre. It was his irony that made him value Shane, a young man who believed in nothing himself, except the reality of the moment and the urgency of his own desires. Tony saw his younger self in Shane, almost the son Susie had stolen from him.

It was only to Shane that he could speak about Fiona, and he was able to do so because he knew that Shane too, being a profound sceptic, was capable of understanding romantic obsession: that since there was nothing permanent in the physical world, a dream was as real as any other experience.

Freddy would have been surprised to know that when Tony abstracted himself from a conversation, and sat with a cigar in his mouth and a balloon of brandy cupped in the palm of his hand between thumb and forefinger, his mind often played with the relation of appearance and reality; astonished to learn that his old mate spent a couple of hours every week reading philosophy. But Tony drew strength from this: from his knowledge that the need for faith, for an absolute Yes or No, was evidence of weakness.

Looking at Andrew Meldrum across the table in the Savoy Grill, he felt his own strength. He said:

'You're not going to stand in my way then.'

There was no question in his voice. Andrew didn't answer for a little, but watched the retreating back of the waiter.

'You make it difficult for me to do so.'

'Difficult, yes,' Tony said. 'Not impossible.'

'Oh well, if we are going to talk about impossibilities, no. You didn't need to do it this way, you know. It's a perfectly feasible, respectable proposition.'

'Then why was your ministry on the point of buggering it up?'

Andrew smiled.

'The contrary proposition was equally feasible and respectable. There were aspects of it which seemed politically more advantageous. That's all. It won't be particularly easy defending the decision to give you the go-ahead.'

'That's your problem,' Tony said.

'As you say . . .'

'And if you said no, you would still have a problem, and a rather nastier one.'

'Yes, you've made that quite clear.'

Tony finished his halibut, pushed his plate aside, and got out his cigar case.

Andrew said: 'I have to tell you that it's not going to be easy persuading my boss that this is the right decision. He was fairly determined to go the other way, you know.'

Tony clipped the end off his cigar and lit it.

'Again, that's your problem. I'm sure you'll find the argument.'

He nodded to the waiter who brought a bottle of Armagnac and brandy glasses.

'Not for me,' Andrew said.

Tony poured out two glasses and pushed one towards Andrew.

'My father was Ukrainian, you know,' he said, 'and it was recognized there that a bargain wasn't concluded till it had been sealed in a glass of brandy. I don't want to find myself doubting your word.'

'Very well.'

He knocked it back, and held out his glass for more.

'That's rather good,' he said. 'You know, you could have got what you want another way. Why did you choose this? And another thing: are you really proposing to run off with my sister Fiona? I must say that was a surprise. I've always been accustomed to thinking of Fiona as a sort of Head Monitor, you know. You can imagine how she disapproves of little me. I know, of course, she had that little run around with some photographer fellow, between you and me, a most unattractive piece of work, but I always thought she had picked on him just to spite our ghastly mother. You won't know her—lucky you—but this chap Kevin was Ma's stud, and so I quite understood that it was rather heaven for Fiona to take him off her. But I thought she'd had her little fling and was now back on the straight and narrow. So it was rather a surprise when you came on the scene.'

'You don't like her, do you?'

'Fiona? No, that's not fair. I neither like her nor dislike her. We don't have much in common, you know. Or I didn't think we did, but now I'm beginning to wonder. Look, if you want to speak about Fiona, and I can see you do, let's go somewhere else. This isn't quite the right ambiance, would you say? Not for confidentialities.'

Tony paused. On the one hand he didn't want to

discuss Fiona with Andrew; on the other hand the temptation was powerful.

'Don't you have to be at the House?'

'Oh, fuck the House.'

They adjourned to a place of Andrew's choosing, a little club in a first-floor room near Covent Garden.

Andrew giggled: 'I suppose it's one thing to be said for blackmail, that one has nothing left to hide from one's blackmailer. This isn't your sort of place, my dear, but it is mine. I spent so many years being careful, you know,'—the tall, slim café-au-lait boy behind the bar greeted him with a light kiss on the cheek—'that it's a great relief sometimes not to have to be. That's a very naughty boy, I'm afraid. I saw your driver here one night. I suppose he was checking up on me, but he seemed to fit in very happily.'

He guided Tony to a table in the corner of the little room, and called for brandies-and-soda.

'I don't think the stuff here can be drunk neat.'

'Shane—that's my driver—prefers girls,' Tony said, 'but he's broad-minded.'

'Rather a nice pun,' Andrew said. 'He didn't give the impression of having broads on his mind the night he was here. I'm sure he'll be welcome any time. No,' he said to the bar-boy, 'no, Jerry, go away, this is a private conversation for the moment.'

'Do they know you're an MP?'

'Why on earth not? So, do tell, are you going to carry Fiona off from her dreary life?'

'You agree it's dreary.'

'Madly, I should say. I thought it suited her, but I mean to say, Gavin. Nobody could stand a lifetime of Gavin.'

Tony hesitated. He felt that in some obscure fashion the tables had been turned: that Andrew had attained the moral ascendancy which had been his at the Savoy. Moreover his disinclination to discuss Fiona had strengthened. She would hate this place. He was almost ashamed to be here and thinking of her.

'She can't make up her mind,' he said.

'Then make it up for her.'

'Gavin's in trouble. You know that. That makes it more difficult somehow. She doesn't want to walk out on him while he's in trouble. On the other hand I can see that she can't stand him.'

'Hasn't been able to stand him for years, ducky.'

He began to analyse the situation. There was nothing new in what he said, nothing that Tony hadn't already guessed. The only surprise was to find how closely Andrew's way of thinking resembled his. He heard the note of resentment of everything which Gavin, or indeed Gavin-and-Fiona, represented, which was familiar to him. Andrew's contempt for it all was radical. It even exceeded his own. He didn't think he felt quite the same venom. But the resemblance was keen enough to be disturbing. Of course he understood its cause in Andrew's case; it wasn't so different from his own. Andrew might have been born within the pale, but his tastes had driven him out. He, too, saw himself as an exile, an Ishmael. Tony looked at his neat trim figure, at the smooth cheeks, the precise mannerisms which in normal circumstances stopped short of the effeminate, but now, control relaxed, allowed his essential womanliness to be evident. And he understood that Andrew was urging him to carry Fiona off, and that this urging was not only an obscure act of revenge, but a sort of wooing. It wasn't that Andrew in any way wanted him, Tony, but that for the moment, in the crepuscular intimacy they had established, Andrew had become, as it were, Fiona.

'She's stifled,' he said. 'I've said I used to dislike her because I thought she was satisfied with that life, but now that she isn't, I feel sorry for her.'

'So you think I've a chance.'

The bar-boy, Jerry, returned and hovered over them.

'I must speak to you, Andy, I need your help, it's a bit urgent like.'

'*Pazienza*, ducky.' He put his left arm round the boy's buttocks and squeezed him.

'Of course you've a chance. Go in and win.'

'But the Gavin problem . . . she does feel an obligation there . . .'

'For Christ sake,' Andrew said, 'you've been ruthless enough with me.'

The boy Jerry slipped onto the chair between them and leaned forward. Tony could feel his sweet creamy breath.

'I don't know what to do, Andy,' he said. 'You must help me.'

'Right,' Tony said, 'I'll leave him to you. Thanks. You've helped me. I'll not forget. Doesn't cancel out the other matter though.'

'I never supposed it would. Right, dear,' he turned to Jerry, 'tell Auntie.'

XV

Liz's festival opened with a concert followed by a champagne and lobster supper (tickets £35 a pair). The concert was held in the Little Theatre she had constructed in their stable block. She had bullied the District Council to back her in this enterprise. The councillors' reward was to appear as patrons of the arts. Many found this flattering. It pleased some of their wives also to present themselves in this guise; others appeared bemused.

This year they required even stronger moral fibre, for Liz had determined to startle them. In the first flush of her enthusiasm for Jason she had agreed that the main item on the programme should be a new dance of his own devising. It was entitled 'The Jazz Hyacinth'—the Greek legend translated to Bondi beach.

'You can hear his imagination creak, rather too audibly,' Colin said, as Jason, all but naked, his body gleaming with oil, pranced through his interpretation of the lovely boy's death at the hands of careless Apollo.

'Bravo, bravissimo,' shouted Rupert Kemsley-Smith, bringing a blush to his father's cheek.

Ginny Prepper rose like the Earth Mother from her chair, clapping her hands above her head.

'I never saw the like,' Margot Rutherford said. 'Mind you, I don't say I'm not glad to have seen it. Once,' she added as if to forestall the possibility of an encore.

'Just a bit on the explicit side for my taste,' Sheena Maconochie said, and then looked round quickly in case this put her out of line with majority opinion. But it was clear that that had not been established.

'Think lover-boy went a bit far?' Liz asked Fiona as she handed her a glass of champagne.

'Oh, I don't know. It's certainly got people talking, and that's always a good thing, isn't it? Was it more or less what you were expecting?'

'To tell you the truth, I was relieved he didn't have an orgasm on stage,' Liz said. 'I'm afraid it's over between us, which prejudices me somewhat. But I'm glad you don't think he went too far.'

'Come off it, Liz. You know you love to shock people.'

'I don't know,' Liz said, 'sometimes I think I'm getting old. There's the bishop, I must have a word with him about the Cathedral concert. He'll have adored lover-boy's act, that's one consolation.'

'Gavin not here?' Gerry Greenheart approached Fiona.

'He didn't feel up to it. He's a bit low . . .'

'They'll treat him with enormous respect in prison, you know,' Dallas Graham said, 'screws and prisoners are all snobs.'

'Well, Dallas, that is helpful. Excuse me, will you . . .'

Caro was standing, withdrawn, half looking out of the window. She seemed near to tears. Fiona touched her on the sleeve.

'I'm sorry,' she said. 'I've been treating you badly. I haven't been able to help myself.'

'Oh Fi . . . I understand. But thanks. I suppose it's been my own fault. Things usually are, aren't they.' She sniffed. 'That dance . . . what did you make of it?'

'Well,' Fiona said, 'well.'

She looked across the now crowded drawing-room. Jason, in a flowered shirt and skin-tight white jeans, was surrounded by admirers. Rupert had his arm round him, hugging him. She saw Ginny Prepper advance. The crowd parted like the Red Sea before her progress. She planted a smacking kiss on Jason's mouth.

'Well,' Fiona said again. 'I don't think it was a cry for help, do you?'

'I hated it,' Caro said. 'It made me feel randy.'

'Oh Caro, please, I wish you wouldn't.'

'I can't help my feelings. And I did say I hated it. . .'

Kenneth sipped his champagne, hoped nobody would come and speak to him, so pretended to be examining the books in the bookcase in the corner of the room. It wasn't a collection which suggested that either Liz or Rory had read anything for years. They were mostly editions from long-extinct bookclubs.

He wondered what Kat would have made of Jason's dance. There had been a letter from her that morning: a cold chill thing, with more about the way German business worked and the way the German economy was moving than about her or him. He turned round to survey the company. Rupert and Ginny Prepper were struggling over Jason's body; that was like another myth, stirring vague memories of Ovid. Perhaps Jason would be transformed into a tree as he stood there, rooted forever to Liz's drawing-room carpet.

The sun was still clinging to the rim of the western hills, pink, gold, crimson, purple, but across the valley the woods were dark. Pheasants congregated on the lawn. A cock took off with a startled clatter, flying low, clumsy, past the grotesque shapes of the two great monkey-puzzles, to the refuge of a larch tree.

Gerry Greenheart came up:

'And what did the young make of that performance, I wonder? A bit exaggerated, I thought . . .'

'Terrible,' Kenneth said, 'simply terrible.'

'You thought that, did you? Severe.'

'Terrible,' Kenneth said again.

'You may have something there. I don't think you've seen my latest acquisition: painting of a monkey and a young girl. Used to belong to Straloch—the old Marquess, I mean. Would value your opinion, Kenneth.'

There was a call for silence. Ginny Prepper, back to the fireplace, was preparing to address the company. She had routed Rupert, and stood with one beefy arm folded round Jason.

'Oh God, she's going to make a speech,' Kenneth said.

'Remarkable . . .'

'I don't know if I can stand this.'

'Friends,' the heavy contralto filled the room. People were subdued, but shifting with premonitory embarrassment.

'This should be good,' Colin said.

'She makes me writhe, literally writhe,' Zoe said.

'Friends, this young genius has given us all an experience to treasure, an insight into the dark mysteries of that world where sex and spirit are entwined. In the beginning there are dark clouds that hang like shrouds over us, hiding the reality of our nature. What do we seek, friends? Let me tell you in one word: we seek release. It is only through release that we can reach out and into our hearts. And what do we find there? We find that storms rock us and mix the men into the women and the women into the men, the past into the present and the future into the past . . . What do we hear? We hear a song. And what is that song, but the song of this mixing. What do we see? We see a dance, a dancer and a dance, and now there is the dance and now there is the dancer and then there is nothing that divides the dancer from the dance, the singer from the song, the teller of the tale from the tale that is told. All is at one, in the union of the thing that is done and the person that is doing it. And that is what this marvellous boy has revealed to us. It is the message of the books I write, which are also and always the books that write me, as this has also been the dance that dances the dancer. Oh be grateful, friends, for the openness of the spirit that is at one with the sex, of the truly unique experience that is always and forever repeated, for the union that is achieved by the locking of the eyes and the dying on the face. The flower is the fruit and the fruit is the flower . . .'

'Bit deep for me that,' Gerry Greenheart said. 'Don't say there's nothing there. Given me an idea indeed. Maybe the monkey is the girl and the girl is the monkey. What do you think?'

'I'd have to see the painting,' Kenneth said. 'But that woman talks a load of crap.'

Ginny Prepper raised both arms on high as if delivering a benediction. Jason was diminished within her enfolding wings.

Nobody knew quite where to look. The sound of sobbing, though embarrassing, was also a relief.

'Oh my God,' Fiona said, 'it's Gavin. He must have come to, and driven over. I suppose I'd better see to the old fool.

'No,' Gavin said, 'don't want to go home. Only just got here. Come to have fun, don't want to go home.'

'But you're not having fun, are you?'

'Not having fun . . .'

With difficulty, and Kenneth's help, she got him out to the car and stowed into the back seat.

'You don't need to come, Kenneth. I don't want to drag you from the party.'

'That doesn't take a wild horse.'

'Sure?'

'Sure. Besides, you'll need me at the other end.'

'I thought I'd just leave him till he comes round.'

They drove through the gathering gloom to the music of Gavin's snores.

When they had got him out of the car, and into the house, and up the stairs, and had deposited him on the bed ('Thank God for downies', Fiona said), they looked at each other and started to laugh.

'I don't know which was worse,' Fiona said, 'Gavin or that awful woman.'

'Oh her, no doubt about it.'

'It's an act of Christian charity on Colin's part, rescuing the niece from that lunatic. D'you know what I would like more than anything? A cup of tea.'

'We haven't talked this summer,' Fiona said.

'We've never talked much.'

'No, my fault I expect, but, still, I thought we were beginning to, but this summer, well it's all been so awful. I liked your Kat, she was one of the few nice things in it.'

'I wish she was "my" Kat. I'm not sure that she still wants to be.'

He gazed into his tea-cup. Fiona studied him: the soft dark hair lying on his brow, the long nose, long upper lip, thin bony hands, the dark eyes concealed under long lashes. He was all elbows and knees and angularities, but the face was distinguished, even if it didn't give promise of energy. She compared it to Tony's. There was sadness there too, she realized, but it was concealed by Tony's vitality. Kenneth's was a suffering face, a Jacobite -in-exile face.

'Look,' she said, 'I don't know her, but I liked what I saw. She's not a girl you can sit back and wait for. You've got to get up and—oh I don't know—fight for her is, I suppose, what I mean.'

'Oh yes, I know that,' Kenneth said. 'Only I don't know how.'

'What you do is your business and God knows I'm in no position to advise anyone about anything. My own life's a mess, as you may realize, but . . . I've always been afraid, Kenneth, that you would just give up, like Colin.'

'It's a temptation,' Kenneth said. He sipped his tea. 'What about old Gavin?'

'Well, yes, that's a problem.'

'Are you going to leave him?'

'I wish I knew. Sometimes I think, yes, I'm almost screaming, and then, I don't know. When I put the downie over him just now, he looked so like Charlie I almost wept.'

'He's my brother, but that doesn't mean much. We've never been able to speak.'

'Poor Gavin, he's never been articulate. I used to say, "thank God", but now I wonder . . .'

'Well, we're none of us good at talking about our feelings,' Kenneth said. 'Actually I despise people who do that sort of thing.'

'Yes,' Fiona said. 'So do I. But I wonder if I'm not making an awful mistake. Kenneth, I've got to tell you something, if you promise that you won't repeat it.'

'Sure.'

155

'She would hate knowing that I'd told you, but I think you have to know. That party of Mansie's, Mansie made a pass at Kat, more than that, tried to rape her actually. I'm sorry, she really didn't want you to know.'

Kenneth got up, crossed over to the window and stood there, his hands resting on the sill. He was bent forward as if the hands were supporting him, and his back was to Fiona.

'I'm sorry if I was wrong to tell you.'

'There's someone out there,' he said. 'Two or three people . . .'

'Oh God, no, let's pretend we're out, or gone to bed.'

Fiona switched off the light.

'They're not that sort of people. They're up to something . . .'

He opened the back door and slipped into the courtyard. He stood still, listening. The footsteps were running now. He heard a shout, then a crash as of breaking glass. A car-engine rumbled into life, and a whoosh of flame rose from the buildings beyond the courtyard, on the other side of the outer wall.

'The stable . . .'

He began to run. He heard Fiona after him. Flames rose before him and the horses screamed in terror. He could hear their hooves too while he was still on the other side of the yard. He threw the door open. A cloud of smoke billowed around him, filling his lungs. The fire danced around him and hurled fantastic shadows of the horses on the wall. He seized a halter, but when he opened the door of the box, he saw that he had no chance of getting it on the pony which was charging round and round in panic. He threw himself at its head and was knocked down. A hoof caught him as he fell. He could hear Fiona in the next box speaking quietly. Then she had got hold of the horse there and was leading it out. Its hooves danced but she got it beyond the fire into the yard. He was on his feet again, and pressed himself to the wall as the pony charged past. Kenneth gasped for breath, and, choking, got the door of the other box open. Scamp,

156

Charlie's Welsh-cross, was whimpering. Kenneth slung the rope round its neck and pulled it towards the door. It reared at the sight of flames, backing away, front hooves flailing. Kenneth held on to the rope. With his other hand he got his dinner-jacket half-off, changed hands and worked the other arm out of its sleeve. He approached Scamp, shortening the rope, and forcing its head still. He threw the jacket over the pony's head, and whipped the rope round its face to hold the jacket in place. Scamp still neighed in terror, but almost blindfold, allowed himself to be eased out of the box towards the door of the stable. As soon as he felt the freedom of the night air, he tore himself from Kenneth's grip and galloped into the darkness. Something hit Kenneth hard on the shoulder, knocking him to the ground. He struggled to his feet, and turning, saw the roof of the stable fall in as flames rose to the sky.

'There can't be any doubt it was arson.'

The fire-brigade had departed, and the autumn dawn was already breaking, mist clothing the lower branches of the trees. Sergeant McGillicuddy sat in the kitchen with Fiona and Kenneth. He tipped a third spoonful of sugar into his tea. The two constables were still outside in the stable yard.

'And I don't suppose there's much doubt as to who's responsible. Were there two men you saw or three?'

'I think there were three,' Kenneth said. 'But I can't be sure. I can't even be sure they were men. They might have been girls, you know.'

'Och no, it'll have been Brogan, there's little doubt of that. He'll have been drinking and then he'll have started talking about Sir Gavin and the accident to his wee girl, and one of his mates will have suggested that the court'll not find a man in Sir Gavin's position guilty. That's the sort of folk they are, Brogan and his mates. And so, they'll have happened on the notion of taking a private revenge. Oh yes, I can just hear them.'

He shook his head.

'They're a sad lot, you ken.'

'But it's so horrible,' Fiona said. 'I can't bear to think of it. The poor horses. If Kenneth hadn't happened to look out of the window and been so quick they'd have burned to death, all three of them.'

'Aye, that they would.'

'What sort of people would do a thing like that?'

'Very ordinary people, very ordinary indeed. They'd have thought you'd all be still at that festival do. They'd not have thought there was any danger of discovery.'

'But would they know about something like that?' Kenneth asked.

'Maybe so, maybe no. I'll have a word with Brogan. I don't think there'll be much trouble laying this at his door.'

'I can understand him wanting to have a go at Gavin. But not the horses, not the horses, that's too beastly. It's not even as if Gavin has anything much to do with the horses. He doesn't even like them.'

'That's no something that would occur to Master Brogan. And he's not very bright, you see. He'd have thought the fire would be put down to an accident.'

XVI

The morning brought no comfort to Fiona. She was up first in the household, and stepped into the yard with the dogs leaping about her. It was the perfection of early autumn, soft, cool, and the air still moist. The trees retained their green, but where the sun, emerging through the mists, touched them there was already here and there a glint of gold and tawny-yellow. But the fresh smells of morning were overlaid with the stench of smoke that still hung over the ruined stable like an evil conscience. She turned towards the paddock and the horses were there, safe, and they had their heads down and were grazing as if last night had not been even a disturbing dream. At least that was something, but she wished she could share their ease of mind. She entered the paddock and called to them, and they came and took peppermints from her, nuzzling her pockets for more, as she felt their legs, trying to ascertain whether any had been damaged in the panic of the night before. They seemed to be all right, but she would have to call the vet over to check them thoroughly. It would be a long time before they could be sure in any case that they hadn't suffered nervous distress. She would be anxious whenever the children rode them now.

She turned back towards the house and felt a reluctance to approach it. She sat on the wall of the little bridge over the burn, and Solomon pushed his face against her legs, while Kirstie and the spaniels searched the shrubbery for rabbits.

'Good boy, good boy'; she fondled the cool velvet ear.

At least she was alone here, for the moment free of other human beings. That couldn't last; the day threatened too many contacts. McGillicuddy might report. There was Gavin, somehow, to be dealt with; he couldn't continue as he was. And Caro must, she realized, be persuaded to leave. That wasn't fair, but Caro, in her unhappiness, was an additional burden she couldn't carry. Fortunately the children were staying with friends and wouldn't be home for a couple of days. That was something.

She lifted her eyes and saw the skeleton of the stable.

It was horrible to think of the hatred that had provoked that. When she had visited the Brogans she had found them sullen and hostile, which she couldn't blame them for being, but she hadn't felt this intensity of hatred that could result in such an action. She supposed McGillicuddy was right, and that it was Brogan. No doubt he had been drunk—'the great Scottish excuse', as she had so often said herself.

She turned away from the house. Two magpies darted out of a beech tree and flew low across the path and out of sight. 'One for sorrow, two for joy'; once magpies had been rare here. Now they were so numerous that you hardly remembered to repeat the old rhyme, or could believe it had any validity.

It had been disconcerting seeing Charlie in Gavin's face last night. She called Charlie 'darling' easily, a word she had never applied to her husband; and she had been pleased, relieved to find him so different from his father, so full of gaiety and vitality and zest. But there: she had seen him in Gavin's face, and couldn't deny it, just as she so often saw herself reflected in Rosie, and disliked her daughter (even while loving her, of course) for that resemblance. There was a line running from Diana through herself to Rosie, which she deplored; but she had thought Charlie free of the malign influence of heredity, as if he had sprung into life miraculously new-minted and untainted. But now—a roe sprang from the undergrowth and bounded off in high leaps— with the spaniels and Kirstie in eager and hopeful-hopeless pursuit—it hadn't, she realized, been Gavin she saw in Charlie, but the other way round, and that made things different. It was as if in that brief glimpse as she put Gavin sodden and revolting to bed, she had caught sight of what had been destroyed in him, of what indeed he had destroyed in himself, a potentiality ruined, never brought to fruition. But that didn't mean Charlie had to go the same way, didn't make any danger mandatory.

'And what of myself,' she thought, 'where do I go? In ten years Charlie will be grown up. And I shan't be fifty. This will all be his, if he wants it, what's left of it, because Gavin . . .'

She leaned over a gate, watching the black cattle, the native breed which many pundits said had had their day, were finished, had no future. They grazed in the morning, in the evening of the breed.

Kenneth dialled the number Colm McStay had given him and was not dismayed when the secretary girl said there was no chance Mr McStay would be in till near lunch.

'And then he'll be out again,' she added. 'You can't know him very well if you think you can catch Colm this early in the day.'

'Well, I'll ring again,' Kenneth said.

'I would say, can he ring you, but he's no good at returning calls either,' she said. 'You've just got to take your chance.'

So he went through to the kitchen and got Mrs Hunter to make him bacon and eggs—with 'lots of bacon, please, and three eggs'.

'That was a terrible thing to happen,' Mrs Hunter said. 'I don't know what the world's coming to.'

But Kenneth looked out on the ruins of the stable with a song in his heart.

'I don't know what you've got to be so cheerful about,' Mrs Hunter said.

'It's a very fine morning, said Mr Drake Puddleduck.'

'I'm sure I don't know what you're on about. Now eat

your breakfast like a good boy. It's nice that somebody in this house has an appetite.'

Kenneth met Fiona in the hall.

'I can't thank you enough,' she said. 'Are you all right? What about your shoulder? I still think we should have it x-rayed.'

'Bit stiff, but fine thanks. How are the horses?'

'They seem to be all right. Kenneth, you look very cheerful.'

'I am, unaccountably. Hope you don't mind.'

'Mind? Why should I?'

'Is there any word from McGillycuddy?'

'Not as far's I know.'

'I liked him. A real Dixon of Dock Green cop.'

'Yes, he's nice. Kenneth, that business of Mansie and Kat. I don't think I should have told you. She didn't want you to be told.'

'That's all right,' he said. 'Bloody silly of her to want to keep it from me. She had me worried. I thought it was something I'd done.'

Fiona took a cup of tea up to Gavin. When she opened the curtains and threw up the window, his eyes blinked and he turned over, burying his face in the pillow in an attempt to regain unconsciousness. But she sat down on the end of the bed, and waited. She waited five minutes till her will prevailed; the birds' song entered the bedroom from the garden and in the distance she could hear the chug of a tractor. These sounds intensified the enveloping silence.

'It's no good,' she said. 'We've got to speak. There's a cup of tea for you there.'

'You said there was nothing to say. I'm not up to it.'

'The stable burned down last night.'

'Christ, I'm going to be . . .'

His body heaved. He leaned over the side of the bed, retching; yellow slime trickled out of the corner of his

162

mouth and fell on the mat. He continued to retch, then lay back, sweating.

'Did you hear what I said? The stable burned down last night. It wasn't an accident. The police—Sergeant McGillicuddy thinks it was Brogan, the father of the little girl . . .'

'God, I feel awful . . .'

'You've got to listen.'

'Take this bloody tea away and bring me a brandy.'

He held out a hand which shook like leaves in a high wind. His face was yellowy white. She wiped his brow with a towel.

'All right,' she said, 'just this once, if it'll help.'

She had to hold the glass for him to drink, but he got it down, and lay back very still and staring at the ceiling as if any movement might disturb the effect of the spirit.

'The first thing is, is the insurance up to date?'

His fingers twitched on the downie cover.

'All right,' she said, 'I can ask Maconochie about that. I suppose it's still his responsibility. The horses are all right, if you're interested. Kenneth and I got them out. Kenneth was terrific.'

'Christ,' he shuddered. His whole body gave a sudden convulsive twitch. 'I think I'm going to die.'

'Oh stop it,' she said. 'Stop it.'

'I'm going to die, I feel like . . . oh God, or I'm going to prison. Don't think I don't know that . . .'

He opened his eyes and looked at her in incredulity and hopelessness, and again, to her horror, she saw the shadow of Charlie in his face.

'I've not been very nice to you,' she said, 'but you've got to make an effort yourself, to face up to things. You can't go on like this.'

'I'd be better dead.'

'We can't go on like this.'

'Far better dead.'

His eyelashes flickered, then the eyes closed. His cheeks were damp. He seemed to drift back into sleep.

She sat there watching him, watching Charlie fade

163

from his face, then flicker back. Then she went downstairs to telephone Maconochie.

Colin drew the cork from a bottle of claret.

'Liquor for boys, liquor for the morning.'

Kenneth was amazed by Colin's mood and appearance: a buoyancy no longer supported by alcohol alone.

'You are really going to be married?'

'Indeed yes, but the slut's not up yet. Nor indeed is Sikes. I could cite him as co-respondent even before marriage. Poor Gavin was in a sad state last night.'

'Sadder today I imagine.'

'Ah well, the Gods are just etcetera. *Und so weiter . . .*'

'I think Fiona's had enough.'

'Perhaps Gavin's had enough of my little sister.'

'I don't know,' Kenneth said. 'I think perhaps he's had enough of life.'

'Or not enough perhaps? It's not that the world is too much with us, as I used to claim, but rather that we can have too little of it. . . .'

'Look,' Kenneth said. 'There's something Fiona told me. Mansie tried to rape Kat the night of his party. I don't know what to do about it.'

'Well, I'm the last person to consult. I don't think I've ever been raped.'

'Be serious.'

'It's impossible to be serious about Mansie,' Colin said. 'It's the sort of thing Mansie does. Sensible people just tell him to bugger off. Only language he understands. What does your girl say about it herself?'

'Well, she may have told him that. Can't tell. Hasn't said anything to me herself, you see.'

'Deep waters. We must consult Zoe. She's the expert, having had a similar experience many times, she tells me, with her Uncle Prepper and others, unnamed.'

He went to fetch her. Kenneth waited in the shabby over-furnished room, admiring, as usual, the stuffed peacock, flanked by Landseers, or perhaps school of Landseers, stags at eve drinking their fill and whatnot.

' "The rose is fairest when 'tis budding new,
And hope is brightest when it dawns from fears . . ." '

He had never thought of Colin as having fears, had always accepted him as he offered himself. But now, he wondered whether there had been fears which new-born hope was banishing.

Did something like that account for his own mood this morning? Or was his own new optimism the result of what had happened last night: the superfluous man become a Hemingway hero as it were. On the other hand, weren't Hemingway heroes themselves super-fluous?

Zoe drifted in, autumn hair tumbled about her shoulders, a towelling dressing-gown (Colin's?) wrapped around her, feet bare and Sikes at her heels. She lay down on the rug in front of the fire in which four or five large logs were burning. She didn't speak till Colin followed with a cup of coffee.

'Now,' he said, 'a question of rape.'

'Bo-ring.'

He explained the situation.

'The question is, I gather,' he said, 'what the girl is likely to feel towards Kenneth here. Does she in some obscure way blame him? Or does she feel tarnished?'

'I guess I always knew Uncle Prepper would stop half-way through. After the first time. But, yes, it sort of puts a girl off. She feels, like, she's just a body. Flesh, you know. It's sorta demeaning to feel you're just flesh.'

165

XVII

The first nip of autumn always made Tony feel good. He had never cared for the softness of summer. Susie was a summer girl; perhaps it was this difference that made them incompatible. But of course it could be explained more simply.

'I'm sorry,' he said to Ted, over a mutton-chop in the last City restaurant to serve that Victorian staple, 'we've got on all right, you and I, after a rocky start, but things have got rockier and rockier between Susie and me. You see, she was always a substitute.'

Ted had come to plead, to try to patch things up.

'You've neglected her,' he said. He frowned. All his life he had dodged moments of emotional difficulty; he hated confrontation. But he adored his daughter; for her sake, he would go through with it.

Tony sympathized with him, and poured him a glass of Burgundy.

'It's no good,' he said. 'Susie cares no more for me than I do for her, Ted. We've been living a lie for years.'

He liked the sound of the sentence, and repeated it.

Ted picked up his wine glass.

'I don't understand,' he said, 'I simply don't understand. Well, I've done my best.'

'I'm sorry,' Tony said again; and he was, to his surprise. He would miss Ted when he would only be glad to be shot of Susie. There had always been a reassuring normality about him.

'I won't make any trouble about the settlement,' he said.

'That's not the point,' Ted said.

*

'She'll sting you, she'll take you to the cleaners,' his lawyer said. 'Have you got the liquidity to satisfy her?'

'Course I have.'

'I hope so. I hope so. I know women like your wife. I've had a lot of clients in your position, Tony. They're always astonished by how much it costs them.'

'I don't care,' Tony said. 'I simply don't care. I just want to be shot of her. . .'

Instead of returning to the office he turned away towards the river. He walked, with his grey overcoat dangling open, his hat pulled over on his brow and a cigar jutting from the corner of his mouth, through the narrow streets burdened with office blocks that destroyed their line and turned unseeing windows on each other. This was his territory, where he was fully himself and master. Even Freddy did not begin to understand how Tony's imagination delighted in the material of their work. Perhaps it was precisely because he was not English that London still excited him. To take a waste site, or a run-down building, or a slice of a stumbling company, and mould it to something vibrant and profitable: it was like sending men into battle. At St Helena Napoleon had brooded on his victories. 'Which was your greatest battle?' they asked him. 'Borodino,' he replied, 'it was magnificent. It was so far from home.' Some historians had seen it as a disaster, but to the Emperor it had remained 'magnificent . . . so far from home'. Tony saw his point.

He reached the river. Looking down its long curve he saw the towers of Dockland rise, majestic, superb, a gambler's throw. He gazed at the rush of grey water, shot with streaks of oily red and yellow. He was deaf to the roar of traffic. Two thousand years ago, a Roman general had stood here, amazed at his distance from Rome; and before him, this had been nothing. Would it be nothing again? No, because something, the knowledge of what had been, would always linger in the anima of the place.

He turned round to see the Tower dwarfed by the Twentieth Century. He had never, in all his years in London, visited it. It was dead, for tourists only, but it had once been the heart of England. He could provide a list of those who had met their death there. It was the sort of thing he knew.

A beggar accosted him, a thin young man in a tattered Army greatcoat, with a wispy beard and a mongrel on a string. Tony gave him ten pounds and a cigar.

'For luck,' he said, but that wasn't the reason for his generosity to beggars, which Freddy disapproved of. Freddy saw them as layabouts, parasites, a burden on industrious men like themselves. Well, of course Freddy was right. They were that, but they were more than that. For Tony they were refugees, the dispossessed of society, men who had no chance of a cigar, even every second Sunday. In recognizing an obligation to them, he did honour to his father; and to all those who had made London something more than one of the waste places of the earth. He had kept this habit from Susie; there would be no need to conceal it from Fiona.

The man hesitated to take the cigar. The neck of a wine bottle protruded from his coat pocket. Tony clipped the end off the cigar and held it out again. This time the man took it, gingerly, as if it was a joke cigar, a trick that might explode in his face. But when Tony passed him a box of matches, he lit it, and held out the matches to Tony. He shook his head.

'Keep them.'

The man moved off without a word of thanks. Smoke curled over his shoulder.

In a wine bar a man in a striped suit was talking urgently into his mobile telephone. Tony knew him, and knew that he had cause for alarm.

He bought himself a glass of tawny port, and sat on a stool at the bar and thought of Fiona. He thought of his enemy: the pity she felt for her husband. 'Love isn't safe when pity's prowling around.' Who had said that? He couldn't remember, and the failure irked him. There had been a time, not long ago, when he had looked at Susie as she set out brisk, coiffured, so carefully dressed, for a meeting, and he had felt a stab of pain as he realized that she was all wrong; that she didn't understand, had indeed no conception of, the gap which divided the appearance she presented to the world and what she thought she was doing in it; that she was blind to the essence of her own being, rooted in comfortable assumptions that the world would always be safe for her. For the first time he allowed himself, now, to wonder if this carapace might not be pierced by the revelation of their failure. But no, she would survive it because she would find no difficulty in holding him and his attitude to life wholly responsible.

He took his second glass of port away from the bar to a table in the corner, and sipped with a new enjoyment. The man with the mobile telephone had gone, and there was now only one other drinker in the little bar: an old man with a white silk scarf loosely knotted, falling away from his adam's apple. He had a black Homburg pushed to the back of his head and his grey moustache was beaded with the sherry he was drinking. He was an old politician, a minister in, Tony thought, the Heath government; now discredited, he dickered about the City, his name on the boards of a declining number of companies, few of them reputable. Now, at four in the afternoon, he sipped brown sherry and talked to himself, his lips intoning a litany of complaint and fear. The burden of his message reached Tony; he was upbraiding mysterious beings, 'the Others', who flourished while things fell away from him. Tony remembered him from twenty years back; assured, complacent, intolerable. He wondered if the old man spent every afternoon in this way.

'Success,' someone had once said, 'is more dangerous than failure.' Were the two so opposed? Didn't the former lead ineluctably to the second? Didn't it indeed sharpen one's awareness of it? Tony thought how

Freddy would be mystified by these reflections. More and more, he found himself using Freddy, his old mate and partner, as a marker in the wilderness they travelled through. The truth was, he no longer, in such moments as the present at least, believed in the reality of success. Perhaps his return to Fiona, the way she had forced herself back into his life, so that her image came between him and other occupations, night and day, was no more than evidence of his dissatisfaction.

He lit another cigar. These thoughts were absurd. He had nothing with which to be dissatisfied, except the realization that when you got what you had aimed for, it didn't matter. But he couldn't believe that of Fiona. Nevertheless, when they were together, he would have to change his way of life. He could see that. He couldn't ask her to live in Surrey while he commuted to the City.

'You're Lubbock.'

The old politician settled himself in the chair opposite Tony. The hem of his overcoat was fringed with saw-dust.

'I'm out of things now,' he said. 'A back-number. But we're heading for a crash. Nobody will listen to me, but that's what's in store for us.'

He talked on, prophesying doom. Tony scarcely listened to the monologue, but heard the wintry malice that was its under-current, like the remorseless ticking of a clock.

At six o'clock, from another bar, he telephoned Fiona. She answered just as he was about to put the telephone down. 'I'll give it three more rings,' he had said, and on the second heard her voice.

'Oh, it's you.'

'Yes, it's me. I've been thinking about you all day.'

'I wish you wouldn't. It's no good.'

'It is. It must be.'

'I don't see how it can be. It's too complicated to explain . . .'

'But it's not, and there's no explanation needed.'

'I can't give any, I've told you that already. Tony, I wish you wouldn't . . .'

'But I have to. We have to. You must see that.'

'Oh Tony, it's no good. Things are too difficult here. I can't think straight.'

'Then leave the thinking to me.'

'Just forget me. You'd be better to forget me. Oh,' she said, 'Andrew rang . . .'. Then the line went dead.

'Oh God,' he said, 'she's exhausted before our journey has even begun.'

He looked round, back at the bar, which was not one where he ever remembered being before. There were half a dozen men sitting there, all in suits, except for one youth in a suede jerkin, who leaned one elbow on the bar, his long fair hair hanging over one side of his angled head. Tony felt a reluctance in the atmosphere of the bar: they were all too close to a home to which they had no desire to return.

He felt too the pleasure of guilt. They would have been looking for him at the office all afternoon. There would have been decisions required of him. They would have telephoned various places where he might be, and tried to call him on the mobile phone which he had dumped, without thinking, in a litter bin by the Tower. They might have sent Shane in search of him. He ordered a large brandy and squirted soda in it. The truth was, none of it mattered, not now. It might matter again to-morrow, but now . . . he hunched his Napoleon-grey coat about him, and gazed at his face in the mirror behind the bar.

The young man in the jerkin was talking, too loudly, about film. Was he trying to sell an idea, or himself? Tony had spent years selling himself, and was tired of it. There must have been days when St Helena was a welcome relief. The man to whom the boy was talking paid no attention. He opened his briefcase, but there was nothing in it but a coloured brochure. Tony felt the pathos of that. He looked at the man, with his untouched pint of beer in front of him, and an expression of boredom or hopelessness on his face; and it seemed to him that he was caught in a movie himself, one of those movies which are all mood, where nothing happens till you feel that nothing can and that everything is dwindling to a halt. The boy put his hand on his companion's shoulder and whispered in his ear, but the man's only response was to lift his own hand and remove the boy's. For a moment he held it by the wrist as if he wanted to maintain some sort of contact, as if that mattered, and then he let it drop. The boy touched his lips with his tongue and looked away.

In another bar, a woman took his arm, and said:

'Come back with me, to my place, my husband's left me, and I'm afraid of loneliness.'

But he shook his head, and detached her, and went out again into the night.

He walked for a long time without purpose or destination. That was strange. He couldn't remember when he had last not known where he was going. He couldn't remember feeling like this, ever. It was as if he was in a lift and it was going down beyond the basement, and he didn't care. That was the remarkable thing. He said aloud, 'and I don't care. . .'

XVIII

Andrew was among those who had been trying to telephone Tony. He started by getting his secretary to put the call through, and then changed his mind, frightened. There are many who would deny the successful an inner life, and colleagues would not have granted one to Andrew, if they had thought about him in that way. He wasn't popular, he knew that; few felt at ease with him or sought him out in confidence. He envied those who had the ability to talk easily and as equals with others. Outside the one milieu where he felt fully himself, which was not however a milieu in which he was prepared to live his life, he grovelled, flattered or bullied. Memories of persecution held him back; he never escaped the small boy who had hidden in lavatories and rhododendron bushes from his tormentors.

It was the small boy who replaced the telephone receiver, relieved that he hadn't been able to get Tony. Then he thought what a fool he had been to try from his office, and went out, leaving his officials with a lame excuse which he knew they didn't believe. He tried two or three times from public call-boxes during the afternoon. Each failure brought him the same relief, the same flicker of self-contempt, a freshening spurt of fear. He knew he had to speak to Lubbock before the news of failure reached him from another quarter, to explain to him that he had done all he could, that he couldn't understand why his Minister had overruled his decision, to beg him to hold his hand. 'It wasn't my fault'; he wanted to scream.

He couldn't face the House. He went to his club, his

respectable club, and thought people were looking at him and discussing him. He retired to the library and tried to make a note of his position, to clear his mind. But it was pointless. His mind was utterly clear. He wished it wasn't. If he didn't reach Lubbock, he had no doubt that Lubbock would carry out his threat, like the brute and school bully that lurked below the surface—and not far below. He had to reach Lubbock and each failure to do so made him more distraught. And yet he was glad not to know the worst. He knew himself very well, and perhaps this was why he . . . It was no good. He left the club and walked in the damp chill of the afternoon away from a future that all at once seemed as cold and inhospitable as the east coast on a day of November haar.

It was also what his Minister had said.

'I don't understand how you can honestly have come to make this recommendation. It reverses everything we have stood for, flies in its face. What possessed you, Andrew? I'm not sure it won't have to be looked into.'

It wasn't only in Andrew's imagination that he had dwelled on the word 'honestly'. He was an old brute, who hadn't wanted Andrew as his under-secretary and would be only too happy to be shot of him. It was like school again: 'Bend over, Meldrum. I promise you this is going to hurt you a damn sight more than it hurts me'.

He thought he had escaped that. But he hadn't. Any more than he could escape that evening in his early twenties when he had been stopped by two young men, his own age, in dirty leather and tattered jeans. He had expected a demand for money, but they identified him instead as what he was, and pushed him and jostled him, and bounced him between them, till one exclaimed, 'Jesus Christ, he's wet himself, the poof's wet himself', and Andrew felt the warmth, and the spreading damp, and the humiliation and renewed terror.

He fled the club and stood in St James's with his raincoat pulled about him, a thin figure, uncertain as a refugee. 'Yes, it'll have to be looked into, you know.' The Minister suspected corruption. But surely he must know what had happened. They must know what he was. In these days when every wretched parliamentary secretary even was subject to positive vetting, they couldn't have had any doubts about him. And yet they had given him the job. There were three members of the Cabinet with the same inclinations as himself, given to the same practices, even if all three of them posed as family men. Well, at least he had never done that, couldn't have brought himself to it. So they thought it was money. They would know different when Lubbock took his revenge.

He would have to resign his seat. It was all legal, what he had done, but they wouldn't be able to accept it being spread all over the newspapers, not even now. The three who shared his tastes would be the loudest voices saying he must go.

Either way he'd had it.

People were looking at him standing there. He didn't flatter himself they'd recognized him. They just thought he was odd. He set off up the hill, then flagged down a taxi.

He directed the man to the little club where he had taken Tony.

'Like a wounded animal,' he thought.

"lo Andy,' Jerry said, 'Fancy something rotten?'

He telephoned Fiona.

'Andrew, this is a surprise. What on earth . . ?'

'Look, do you know where Lubbock is?'

'Of course not. Why should I?'

'Oh, come off it, little Sis. Thing is, he's gone missing, just when I have to speak to him, and I thought that perhaps . . .'

'What is all this? You don't sound yourself. You sound agitated.'

'I'm all right, but, if he telephones . . .'

'Not likely . . .'

'You don't need to pretend. I know what's going on between you. So listen. When he telephones would you

175

please tell him that I've been trying to get hold of him. Things have gone wrong. Tell him that, and say I must speak to him before he does anything, and it's not my fault. Have you got that? It's not my fault.'

'All right, I'll tell him. I don't understand but I'll tell him and are you sure you're all right?'

'Yes, of course.' He nestled the receiver between his jaw and shoulder and stretched out his hand to take hold of Jerry by the upper arm. The boy was wearing a T-shirt, and Andrew fondled the cool café-au-lait flesh. 'Why shouldn't I be all right? It's just rather urgent, that's all.'

'Okey dokey, where can he reach you?'

'On my mobile.'

'Mobile?'

'Mobile telephone.'

He gave her the number.

Jerry said: 'That Shane was in again.'

'Was he looking for me?'

'Didn't say so.'

He detached himself and crossed over to the juke-box. In a moment the voice of Elvis singing 'Wooden Heart' flooded the mean room.

'Want to dance?'

'Not dance, no.'

He took the boy in his arms. A little later some other people came into the club and Jerry went to serve them. Andrew picked up a *Standard*. There was an item in the Stop Press: 'Financier found shot: Frederick Paynter (42), a director of Lubbock-Paynter Investments and associated companies was found shot in his office today. Police enquiries are continuing. The Serious Fraud Squad is reported to be investigating the group of companies.'

Andrew read it twice. There seemed to be no other words in the paper. He sat back, biting his nails. Poor bugger. Mansie Niven had once said to him: 'You can stick anything out if you choose to. You know my motto where blackmailers are concerned. Make them commit suicide.' Well, Paynter hadn't as far as Andrew knew been a blackmailer himself, he might not even have been

176

privy to what Lubbock was up to, but all the same . . . poor bugger. At least it meant that Lubbock would have other matters on his mind besides revenge . . . or Fiona. So where did it leave him himself? It was worse than it had been, for sure. There was no way now, no conceivable way in which he could keep his job. That was certain. It was bad enough to have made that recommendation on the Aylesbury affair in defiance of agreed policy. When the company he had backed proved to be subject to an investigation by the Serious Fraud Squad, which was knowledge he had shied away from, in his fear, well . . . On the other hand, Lubbock would now have nothing to gain from carrying out his threat. Except the pleasure of revenge. Andrew had an uncomfortable feeling that Lubbock might enjoy revenge, might want to bring everything crashing down with him.

He telephoned Fiona again.

'This is getting monotonous. He rang. I've passed your message.'

'No, but, listen. Something's happened. I've just learned that his partner has shot himself and that the firm is being investigated by the Fraud Squad. Will you assure him I had nothing to do with that.'

'Why should you have? Why should he think you have?'

'It's complicated, but tell him that. Please, Fiona.'

He had to speak to him, but he didn't want to. He wanted to run, but he didn't know where, and he knew it was the last thing he should do.

'Jerry, sweet, when are you off this evening?'

XIX

'Hear you're getting married, sir.'

'That is correct, Angus.'

'Congratulations. Hope you'll be very happy. Sorry we won't see as much of you here, but that's marriage. We don't see so much of the married gentlemen, not till things start going wrong, that is, and then I sometimes say we see too much of them. Still, look on the bright side, you'll have someone to leave the dog with, sir, when you feel like looking in. I'm sorry to say we've had more complaints about his presence. Mr Maconochie for one is very strong against dogs in the club, says they're as bad as passive smoking.'

'You don't want to listen to a young shit like Maconochie, Angus,' Colonel Greenheart said.

'I try not to, sir, I try not to, but he's very persistent. He's been talking of raising the matter in committee.'

'Cheek,' the Colonel said, as Angus disappeared into the little room at the back of the bar where he prepared sandwiches. The Colonel pushed Sikes with his foot. 'Good dog. It's time young Maconochie got his come-uppance.'

'I think he may have,' Dallas Graham said. 'He was looking very white about the gills when I saw him earlier today. How's old Gavin's case going, Colin?'

'Who can tell? Sikes and I have been about this matrimonial business.'

'Must tell you,' the Colonel said. 'Had an idea. Not something that happens often, but might be a pleasing one. Would your good-lady-to-be care for that painting of the monkey and the girl as a wedding present? She seemed very taken with it when I showed it her.'

'Zoe has an enquiring mind.'

'Thought of giving it to the nation, but what's the nation done to deserve it? Damn all.'

'Sikes would be very grateful too.'

'What has that absurd woman got that I haven't?'

When Liz had telephoned, suggesting lunch, Fiona had hesitated. She was fond of Liz but the old thing was known as the greatest gossip in the county, and Fiona wasn't sure that she could stand having her life picked over for Liz's amusement. It was going wrong in too many places, she thought. But now it seemed as if it was Liz who was near to tears, and she was glad she hadn't said no, though really she had only agreed because Gavin had an appointment with his new lawyers and in his strange new state of mind was refusing to drive himself.

'I mean,' Liz said, 'I know that Rory and me, well, we're not the brightest and you couldn't ever say it was a Great Romance, but then we're neither of us built for Great Romances, I've always said, and we have rubbed along well enough for yonks.'

'Always thought you the couple-est couple I know.'

'There you are then.' Liz poured herself more wine. The bottle was going down fast and Fiona hadn't drunk more than half a glass. 'I'm beginning to think there's something wrong with me. First, lover-boy. Well, that was no surprise. I mean, I never thought of that as more than a passing fling. Well, you couldn't, not with someone of that sort. But I didn't know then of course he was quite that sort of that sort that he's proved to be.'

'Well,' Fiona said, 'I had my doubts from the first moment I saw him.'

'Clever of you. I suppose I was blind. Even so, it's the first time I've ever been tossed aside for a little runt like Master Soppy Smith.'

'Ruby-lips, Colin calls him. Not that that means anything.'

'All the same, it's Rory that bugs me. What does he see in the woman?'

'She's grotesque.'

'Precisely. And he can't really believe she thinks he's the reincarnation of Bothwell.'

'Well, you know how he ended up.'

'No I don't. You forget I'm not educated like you.'

'Mad and chained in a dungeon. I used to think it so sad. In Denmark, I think it was.'

'Served him right, I daresay. And then the woman talks about Rory playing a Highland laird in a TV adaptation of some piece of tosh she's written. Rory. I ask you. If you ask me it's that ghastly Enid we have to thank, for bringing her here. Crazy. Look, love, I feel like getting plastered. If I order another bottle, will you drive me home?'

'Don't forget I've got to pick up old Gavin. It makes him nervous, seeing people plastered, now.'

'Is he really on the waggon?'

'Well, he's trying to be. Mind you, I don't say he's not taking the odd snifter in his business-room. There's a whiff about him sometimes. But he is trying.'

'Poor Fiona. You are brave. Sorry to hear about Andrew by the way.'

'Oh Andrew, yes, I don't know what's going to happen to him. It's funny, how much it mattered to him being a Minister, even a junior one. I mean, when Mansie's thing blew up and he had to resign from the Scottish Office, well, water off a duck's back. But Andrew's really cut up, I think. He's run away of course. Typical.'

'Poor Andrew. I've got a soft spot for him, you know, despite everything.'

'Yes, I know.'

'I rather fancied him once, you know.'

'Yes, Liz, I know.'

'And what about your chap? He seems to be in some sort of trouble too.'

'Deep trouble. But he's not my chap. Anyway how did you know about him?'

'Oh, you can't keep a secret in Perthshire . . . you

ought to know that. And Colin's really going to get hitched to that weird girl?'

'Looks like it.'

'It's an act of charity of course taking her away from that gorgon. All the same.'

But really, Fiona thought, as she poured Liz into the back seat of the car and prepared to collect Gavin, it's too much. What have I done, I mean? But then what has poor Liz done? I suppose she's made a joke of Rory all these years, and thought he liked it well enough, and now along comes this Ginny Prepper and takes him as someone absolutely serious, and he thinks it's wonderful. Well, I've never subscribed to the joke theory myself, that after all is why Colin drives me so mad, but all the same, poor Liz, who was now snoring.

Gavin made no comment on her presence, even when Fiona said that she thought, all things considered, Liz having such a rough time and everything, they'd be better to take her home with them and have her stay the night, even if it was only afternoon now, because she'd feel so bloody when she woke and to be all alone in that house, full of Rory and empty of Rory, a bit too much, what did he think?

But it seemed he thought nothing. He sat there in a sort of stupor, with a little timid smile on his face, and occasionally pulling at his moustache, so that if she hadn't collected him direct from the lawyer's where she had deposited him, and if there hadn't been any smell, not the merest whiff, of alcohol, she'd have thought he'd gone to that club of theirs and got quietly sozzled.

'How did it go then?' she said.

He hated direct questions, always had, but there were times when you had to if you wanted to know anything.

But he looked out of the window, and she was reminded of how he had irritated her in the early years of marriage, before she bit his head off and stopped him, by his habit of commenting on the condition of the crops or the cattle in every field they passed, and it had taken her

181

ages to realize that he didn't really know a damn thing about it, and that his opinions were quite worthless on such matters as—she had soon been forced to think—on everything else, the silly old chump.

At last he spoke. He spoke in that new voice he had acquired since what she thought of as his disaster. It was a voice that she couldn't yet associate with him, though clearly if he was going to stick to it, she was going to have to, assuming that was that she was going to stick with him, which was a matter, resemblances to Charlie sleeping or not, that she hadn't yet resolved on. If she did, this voice, if it lasted, which it might not, would take some getting used to, because at the moment it made her want to scream; it was so odd and distant and not belonging. Of course old Gavin had always been vague, vagueness itself, but this was more than vague or worse than vague, it was sort of dislocated, almost, if not quite, the sort of voice they gave creatures from other worlds in those awful space movies that Rosie, inexplicably to Fiona, had become addicted to. She hated the word 'addicted' and the thing it represented. One of Gavin's merits, once, had been that he was so vague he wasn't addicted to anything. That was before the gin of course.

'Well,' he said, 'it's complicated', making that not very difficult word sound as if it had been dredged up from the depths of the dictionary.

His narrative lasted all the way home, in its disjointed hard-to-follow fashion. Gavin had always told a story as if he had got it wrong; he was worse now; he would be worse still when it came to going into the witness-box. They should get him to plead guilty.

Anyway he had seen two partners, the one who was handling the estate business which they were trying to take out of Maconochie's hands, and the one who was taking charge of the motoring case.

'Not very hopeful, not bloody hopeful at all. Lack of . . . what did he say, mitigating—that the right word, Fi?—circumstances. Well, could have bloody well told him that myself. Don't think he likes me.'

182

'It doesn't matter whether he likes you or not as long as he does his job properly.'

As for the estate business, that was complicated too, because Maconochie declined to surrender the files till his firm's account had been settled in full.

'But these chaps say we should dispute it.'

Then there was something funny going on. Gavin didn't understand it, so that Fiona wished she had gone along with him despite his reluctance, but it seemed that it concerned the sale of the farms which Maconochie had been handling. As far as she could gather, the sale had fallen through, but there was some reason to suppose that Maconochie had been acting in a dodgy manner, for both sides in the transaction.

'Hares and hounds, y' know,' Gavin said, and fell asleep.

'He telephoned,' Caro said. 'He wasn't pleased it was me that answered,' she added with what seemed to Fiona like satisfaction. 'He's in trouble, you know, he's in worse trouble than Gavin.'

Fiona, depressed by the malice in Caro's voice, didn't answer, but pushed past her sister-in-law, and through the lobby and out of the house again by the back door, heading for the temporary stables where Kenneth was helping Charlie and Rosie to tack up the ponies.

'If you wait a bit,' she said, 'till I've had time to change, I'll come with you too. Kenneth, why don't you come with us. Take old Crusader, you haven't ridden for ages.'

'No clothes.'

'Jeans'll do. Crusader's very quiet, you know.'

There was still warmth in the sun as they trotted up the winding path through the wood, pursued by the angry clamour of a jay, breaking the deep stillness of the pines. Reaching the moors, they saw the sun still high above the western hills. But the lochan was already in the shadow of the pines and black as the mood which the ride had lifted from Fiona. They disturbed a heron from its priestly fishing, and it flew away with heavy sepulchral beating of its wings.

'It's seven years bad luck to shoot a heron,' Charlie said. 'Isn't that true, Mummy?'

'Stupid, you've got it mixed up with breaking a mirror, stupid,' Rosie said.

'Oh, I'm sure it's awfully bad luck to shoot a heron,' Fiona said.

'It's wicked, but it's not bad luck,' Rosie said. 'They're not the same, Charlie.'

'Race you to the Trig Point,' Charlie said, and the children galloped off.

'Well, they're all right,' Fiona said. 'It's good to be here. It's been too long.' She bent forward and clapped her mare on the neck. Then she held her hand wet with the horse's sweat to her nostrils. 'We should do this more often,' she said.

'I'm glad I came,' Kenneth said, 'but I won't be able to again for a bit.'

They dismounted, and sat on a broken dyke over the lochan, holding the reins loosely and letting the horses graze the coarse pale-green grass.

'I'm going to London,' he said. 'I've got a job, well, a sort of job. You know I've been trying to get hold of Colm McStay because he promised to try to help. Well that was no good, but a friend of mine, Rashid, is starting a magazine and he wants me to work for him.'

'But that's super,' pleased for him, certainly, but knowing dismay also. 'I'll miss you of course, but that's terrific. What sort of magazine?'

'Oh this and that, satirical mostly. It'll probably flop, but Rashid's rich enough to carry it for a bit. His father owns half of Lucknow or somewhere. There's a lot of money in being a slum landlord in India, it seems. I'm to be an assistant editor or something.'

'It's a start,' Fiona said, 'that's the great thing.'

'Oh yes, I suppose so.'

'But I'll miss you. Ever since the fire I've realized . . . but that doesn't matter. Have you told Kat?'

184

'Not yet. I wanted to tell you first. See what you thought.'

'But that's obvious. It's super. It'll strengthen your position enormously.'

'I'm not so sure. She can't stand Rashid, you know. But I've got to do it.'

'The great thing is, it's a start. It's so much easier to move to another job when you have one, I'm certain of that. Perhaps your McStay chap will be better able to help you when you've got what they call a track record.'

'Maybe. I think he's more talk than help actually.'

'There are a lot of people like that,' she said, thinking of several among whom, in her present mood, she included herself.

'But I don't like to leave you the way things are.' Kenneth lit a cigarette and lay back. 'Will you be all right?' he said, not looking at her.

She watched the smoke drift up, blue till it mingled with the soft air around the water.

'Sweet of you,' she said, 'we'll get by. I wish Caro would go though.'

'I thought you liked having her here. I thought you get on so well together.'

'We did, but haven't you noticed, we don't now, it's become awkward having her about. Don't ask me why and for God's sake don't ask her, or let her know what I've said. Promise.'

'Promise. Anyway, I think I understand. I've been blind not to see it. But what about old Gavin? Are you going to ditch him?'

'Oh God, I don't know. I wish I could, but how can I, with all this hanging over him. And he's so pathetic the efforts he's making now, when they're at least two years too late. It's terrible. I admire them of course, but they irritate me so. He just gets on my nerves, whatever he does. I couldn't say this to anyone but you, Kenneth. And that's not the worst of it.' She paused. She looked at his profile etched against the sky, at the smoke rising, and beyond it, at the hills which were now darkening as

185

the sun began to sink. 'There's Tony. You know who I mean?'

'Caro's spoken about him.'

'Oh yes. He's in trouble too. He's been knocked off his perch, and that's made me realize I'm crazy about him, all over again. And it's hopeless. I can't stop thinking about him and it's hopeless.'

XX

A wisp of hair rested on her lips. He blew it away, and leaning across he touched the lips so lightly with his own that it was scarcely a kiss, but yet enough of one to draw from her a murmur in which there was no dissent, no complaint, but only content like music on the waters. The moist warmth of her body lay against him, but with him, his in surrender, as his was hers also, and his right hand rested between her thighs, his thumb tickling and tickled in her bush. The late afternoon sun slanted in, turning the standard issue hotel dressing-table a rich ruby. The noise of traffic sounded far away, which it wasn't, except in his mind.

When he had telephoned, urging, she had said, no, it was impossible, there was no sense, it could only pain them both, for there was no future. Had it been something in his voice, rather than the words he employed, which had persuaded her to consent, still protesting that she could not? And was it the promise of pain for both that gave him hope and had thus given him the strength to continue his urging? For, if the meeting threatened pain for both, that admission told him what he wanted to know; and so made their meeting even more imperative.

She looked more beautiful than ever when she rose from the sofa in the hotel lobby. That look of assurance which came from her not knowing was gone; he had adored it, it had drawn him to her, for it had made her vulnerable; but its absence deepened her beauty and refined it. The wound, sword-gash, stabbing spear, had been inflicted. They were equals, he thought, as they had never been. The match was complete.

187

She ate little at the lunch which in the necessary pretence that this was still somehow a social occasion they took in the hotel dining-room: a few slices of smoked salmon, a glass of hock, a salad, two cups of coffee. They talked little too; the lunch was like those premonitory snatches of action which directors fashionably indulge in to tease the audience before the credits roll and the movie gets under way.

Very gently, he disengaged his cramped left arm on which her head had been resting, did so without disturbing her more than to elicit another cat's purr of soft content, and stretching to the bedside table, found a cigarette (Gitanes, no filter), and lit it. He drew smoke deep into his lungs and expelled it in a blue-grey dissolving cloud.

Such blue-grey clouds of French soldiers were scattered over the Russian wastes as the Army withdrew from Moscow. After the horror of the crossing of the Beresina came *la dégringolade, la débâcle*, until one day early in January 1813, the proceedings of the City Council of Warsaw were disturbed by the irruption of a red-headed scarecrow, blackened with gun-powder and dirt of travel; when they asked who this creature in tattered uniform was, and what he meant by breaking in on them, he drew himself up, and replied '*Je suis la Grande Armée*', for it was indeed Marshal Ney, the cooper's son, the last man to cross the Niemen out of Holy Russia, the only man in that Army of 600,000 men who, unlike the Emperor, two Kings, a Prince, and eight Marshals, had not been defeated.

And on account of this memory Tony had always felt a special reverence for Michel Ney. Whenever he was in Paris, he would find some opportunity to stand before his statue near the Closerie des Lilas and bow his head in memory. Hemingway, he recalled, had felt the same way about Ney, and he often wondered if it was the Marshal who had supplied Hemingway with that line, which Tony also revered and kept by him as a talisman: 'Man can be defeated, but not destroyed'.

It was a line poor Freddy had never learned, and so, overwhelmed by their defeat, Freddy had destroyed himself. Tony regretted him, missed him, and despised and condemned his action.

'I have to tell you,' he said, 'My situation's desperate. It's as bad as the Battle of Leipzig.'

She sat by the window, her hair wet from her shower and lying on her shoulders, and she wore a white towelling dressing-gown with the hotel monogram on the breast.

He opened a half-bottle of champagne from the mini-bar, and handed her a glass, leaning over to kiss her lips, but not spilling the wine.

'I don't know about that,' she said.

'Otherwise called "The Battle of the Nations". Napoleon was outnumbered two to one, and the battle lasted three days, and when it was lost, he was all but finished. There was only one bridge out of Leipzig and the order to build pontoons had either not been given or had gone astray, and then even the one bridge was blown up with twenty thousand men on the wrong side. Well I'm not sure I'm not one of those marooned on the wrong bank of the River Pleisse with no hope of escape.'

'I knew you were in trouble,' she said. 'That was really why I came when I said I wouldn't. But I didn't know it was so deep. This hotel? Can you pay for that, or would you like me to? I could, easily. Let me.'

'Thanks, but a drop in the ocean. Besides, I've still got bits of plastic—Diner's Club, Amex, they haven't got round yet to taking them away. Besides,' he said again, 'I'm oddly still in the state of having some money coming in which they are allowing me to use.'

'I don't really understand it,' she said. 'Do you want to tell me . . .'

So he did. He didn't try to make the best of it, or gloss over anything. He had taken chances, and they hadn't come off, but if they had, he would have been all right. It was a matter of corner-cutting, he said, but if you were stopped before you regained the main road, then it counted as dishonest. He hadn't been charged yet; but he had no doubt he would be. They would call it theft and false accounting, though it was (essentially) their own money that he and poor Freddy would have been accused of stealing, and if things had worked out fine, the accounting would have been no more than creative.

The market had turned at the wrong moment. Their ventures had been too ambitious, as rash as the invasion of Russia. But that was always the danger when you aimed high.

He was sorry, by the way, about her brother.

'Andrew's terrified of you,' she said. 'He's been on the telephone again begging me to get you to hold off.'

'All I did was threaten him,' he said, 'to get him to lend his weight. Now . . .' he drank some champagne, 'now there's no point in doing what I threatened to do. That would just be revenge, and I'm not interested in revenge.'

She looked at him. He turned away so that she couldn't see how her look affected him.

'Poor Andrew,' she said. 'He doesn't understand you, he's really terrified.'

'Well, you can tell him to rest easy. I'm not interested in Andrew. It's us that matter. You and me. What about us?'

He wished she would meet his eyes. If she looked at him and he held her gaze, she couldn't say no.

'Things are different,' he said. 'I can't buy you now. I can't offer you anything better than what you ran away from when we were young?'

'And we're not young, now. Why should you hope I'm braver than when we were young?'

'You are braver. I know that.'

'And if I am, that still doesn't mean . . . because there are other things now, you know.'

'Yes,' he said, 'you're confined now, held by obligations, your children, I understand that. And I'm going to prison, almost certainly.'

190

'So's Gavin,' she said. 'So's Gavin.'

He had a ridiculous picture of her commuting between the two prisons, sitting lost and lovely and too carefully-dressed, in suitable visiting gear, at a little table and conversing first with one, then with the other, through a grille. Probably it didn't happen like that now, but that was the picture that presented itself to him.

'I thought I could buy you,' he said. 'I don't mean the straight cash offer I made to your husband. That was a joke or almost only a joke, but I was in communication with his lawyer about these farms he was selling. I was going to buy them and then, when the deal was done, I thought I'd be able to say, "Look, I've got your husband out of his financial mess. That sets you free. So come to me." Does that sound ridiculous?'

'Utterly.'

She smiled.

'Utterly,' she said again. 'I'd no idea you were so romantic. It sounds so operatic. It wouldn't have worked though.'

'No? Why not?'

'Because it just couldn't. Not done like that. If you can't see why, I'm sorry. You'll just have to take my word. Tony, do you always think things must be just the way you want them?'

'Sure,' he said. 'Secret of my success,' and laughed.

'Because they can't be,' she said. 'What about your own marriage? Why did that go wrong?'

'Because Susie wasn't you,' he said.

'That's nonsense. I bet when you married her you didn't even think of me. You're not telling me you stood at the altar—it was a church wedding, I suppose—saying to yourself "this is the wrong girl coming up the aisle".'

He had to laugh at that; even so, the night before it, he had got drunk with Freddy and told him, again and again, it was all a mistake and he wished he was out of it. But he couldn't say that now, to Fiona.

'Of course not,' he said. 'I always knew I'd accepted second best, but I thought I was realistic about it. And I

191

really fancied Susie. No problem there, then. Only, it was corrupted from the start, long before she began to disapprove of me and of the things she thought I was doing in business. She used to say I was immoral.'

'In what way?'

In what way? That charge, so often levelled, had come to annoy him more than anything about her, if only because she had never hesitated to accept the results of what she condemned.

'She didn't know anything about the business, or want to know. Fair enough. That didn't worry me. No, it went deeper. She thought me immoral because I tell the truth. . .'

'Oh Tony, come off it.'

'It's true. There's nothing so immoral in some people's eyes as telling the truth. Susie lived in a cloud of cant. She was as selfish as they come and yet she never admitted that self-interest, self-gratification are the motivating forces in life. She preferred things to be pretty. She used words to deceive herself and others . . .'

'And what makes you think I don't?'

'Because you're not a coward.'

'Oh, but I am. And why do you say that? You thought me a coward years ago, you found me out then . . .'

Her voice trembled. She was close to tears. If she broke down, he was lost.

'No,' he said. 'No. But you're too scrupulous. Live all you can; it's a mistake not to.'

'People mean such different things by life,' she said.

He had flown north with nothing to offer but himself and what he knew was between them. All the way he had told himself this was enough. In bed, making love, he had felt sure: she couldn't say no after that music.

'If this was a romantic novel,' she said, 'if only it was . . .'

A speech formed in his mind:

'I need you. Don't you see that behind the front I'm offering, I'm as naked and lonely and afraid as my father when he fled from the Ukraine? Don't you see that I'm a refugee too? We've talked of courage, your courage, but what about mine? I don't know if I have the courage to go on without you. I don't even know if I want to. Oh, I admit I'm not going to take Freddy's way out, but I'm afraid all the same to live, diminished, deprived. We're none of us—I've learned this—able to go through it all alone. We need the assurance of loving and being loved. Without that it's as if we're trapped in a dark wood, and there is no path out. I've cut my hands once on the briars seeking a way through. I don't know that I have the strength to do it again . . .'

But he didn't say any of this, of course he didn't, and he even smiled at the thought that he might have.

'I wish things were different,' she said.

'Yes, I've nothing to offer you. I thought I had so much and it's crumbled in my hands.'

'It's not that,' she said. 'If it was only that, it would be easy. I'm not afraid of that now. You were right, I was before, and I despise myself for it. But it's not that. It's other people. You said: "live all you can, it's a mistake not to"; and you're right. I know that now. For a long time I didn't. Maybe it would have been better if you had turned away when you saw me sitting in that hotel, better for you, Tony. But it's been good for me that you didn't. I was low then, I thought I was worthless. You've changed that. But I can't come with you. There are too many other people who will be hurt if I do. Gavin's put up with a lot from me, over the years, I see that, and I owe him something. It's a debt I don't want to have to pay, but must. Please understand. And if I was to abandon him and the children and duty . . .'

'I never asked you to abandon the children.'

'No, of course you didn't, but . . . it's no good, that's all. I would feel so guilty and that would corrupt everything we might have. But now we'll always have it—today, this afternoon, for ever . . .'

'I've heard that line before,' he said. 'I've even used it. I never believed it then.'

'The terrible thing,' she said, 'is that what was wrong

193

before is the only thing I can do now again. Oh God, I'm going to cry . . .'

Later she drove him to the airport to catch the last shuttle. Lights flashed off the wet road. When he had waited in the queue and checked in and got his boarding pass, he kissed her, and told her not to wait.

'This is a terrible place to say good-bye, and I hate good-byes anyway.'

'I hate airports,' she said.

She looked at the screens.

'But you're not called yet. I'll wait. It doesn't have to be goodbye, not like last time.'

'No,' he said, 'not like last time.'

'I'm not going to let you go like last time. There's no need. And you'll let me know what's happening.'

'The papers will do that, if anything happens. But, yes, I'll let you know. I'll have to. Even if you wanted it I couldn't make a clean break. Not again.'

'Tony,' she said, 'there's one thing. One thing you should know.' She slipped her arm round his waist. 'If you'd stayed on top, if you'd brought off all your deals and set Gavin up again, it wouldn't have worked. I'm not for sale. I'd made up my mind that time we went fishing. You must believe that.'

'Then all this,' he said, 'what's it? Pity?'

'No, Tony, not pity. Love, love of a sort, all I'm capable of, not enough perhaps, but all . . .'

She brushed his lips, turned away, through the automatic door and out into the night. He watched her till she was out of sight, and then headed for the departure lounge. He bought a large brandy, and holding it in his hand, paced up and down as if on the deck of a ship, his overcoat swinging open. He leaned against the rail by the window and drank the brandy and watched the rain bounce off the tarmac. Called on to surrender as they withdrew from the Field of Waterloo, the Commander of the Guard answered: *'la Garde meurt, mais ne se rend pas'*.

XXI

It was the cool crisp of autumn, and you had to step out to keep warm, but the wind which had blown strong for three days and nights had died away, and the sky was a deep true blue with the pines black against it. Colin had paid to have oil-fired heaters installed in the little church.

'Don't want a frozen bride. Southern gal, you know,' he told the new recently-appointed rector, the Rev Francis Snaith-Seath, who looked like one of nature's blind alleys and whose behaviour was already said to confirm this impression.

'It's my first marriage,' the rector said.

'I'm ahead of you then, old hand at the game.'

'Of course I don't really approve of divorce, un-canonical in my opinion, but then, marriage isn't really my line either.'

He poured himself a second glass of the champagne, which Colonel Greenheart, in his capacity as best man, had had waiting for them in the vestry.

The church was filling up. 'Tout le monde' as Enid Kemsley-Smith put it, was there. This was not quite correct. Gavin was missing, having been refused leave-out from the jug. It was uncertain whether Ginny Prepper herself would appear; she had suffered an unfortunate accident at Fotheringay, twisting her ankle as she stepped backwards over a ruined wall in an attempt to drink in the atmosphere. But Mansie Niven was there, garbed as a seventeenth-century Highland Chief with an eagle's feather in his bonnet. And young Straloch was there, in sandals and tattered jeans, a black girl in attendance.

'Pity that chap Lubbock isn't here,' Bill whispered to his wife as he surveyed the gathering congregation. 'It would have given him a truer idea of Scotland, nature's democracy.' He pointed to Straloch. 'I mean look at that chap there. Might be a beggar. Still, "a man's a man for a' that".'

'Yes, dear,' Lou said, 'but Lubbock's going to prison, isn't he? I daresay he'll find all sorts there too.'

'How true,' Dallas Graham spoke up from the pew behind. 'The two nicest chaps I met in the nick were a black burglar from Wapping called Andy and a blind Wykehamist blackmailer.'

'Whisht,' Sergeant McGillicuddy dug him in the ribs. 'There are folks trying to say a wee bit prayer.'

'Oh that still goes on, does it,' Dallas said.

'I'm so glad you could come,' Fiona said to Kat as they approached the church. 'I was afraid we were going to lose you after . . . Kenneth was very down, you know. He has warned you Mansie will be here, hasn't he? There was no way he couldn't be asked.'

'That's all right.'

'Good, you do make a nice pair. The last wedding I went to in this church was my own. Isn't that awful?'

'I'm sorry about Sir Gavin.'

'Oh well . . . poor old thing, weddings aren't his style anyway. Did I tell you, Kenneth, that bloody Brogan has an alibi?'

The strains of Saint-Saëns' 'Softly Awakes My Heart' from *Samson and Delilah* greeted the arrival of the bridal party. Zoe had striven to look an ordinary bride; not successfully. Caro was one bridesmaid, Rosie the other. Charlie acted as page, leading Sikes.

'He absolutely refused until he was told that Sikes was to be the other page,' Fiona whispered.

'Wouldn't be right not to have Sikes,' Margot Rutherford remarked. 'Some people say dogs are out of place at weddings. Can't see it myself.'

*

As Zoe arrived by Colin's side, all eyes were diverted to the door, which had opened again to admit Ginny Prepper, hobbling between crutches, and supported by a white-moustached gentleman in the uniform (known to all on account of *Gone With the Wind* and other movies) of a Confederate Colonel, Rupert Kemsley-Smith in a black velvet suit, Jason, and Rory looking sheepish.

'The rector tried to ban Sikes,' Fiona whispered. 'He hadn't a chance. Rory looks pretty desperate.'

The music stopped, the ceremony got under way. No one advanced any reason why these two should not be joined in Holy Matrimony. Colonel Greenheart produced the ring, examined it as if assessing its value, and handed it over. Sikes sat down and scratched himself, then, drawing a resisting Charlie after him, advanced on the rector who gave a shrill yelp and scurried for the vestry.

'I think he's completed the job,' Colin said. 'However we must follow him to sign the book. I don't think Sikes should come, Charlie. He seems to disturb the rector.'

'I can't bloody well stop him,' Charlie said.

Zoe knelt down by the dog.

'Sikes, you may kiss the bride. I adore them, they have no clue,' Colin said.

But clueless or not Sikes did as he was bid.

Mansie, glass in hand, approached Kat and Kenneth,

'No hard feelings, I hope.'

'I have,' Kenneth said.

'Wasn't talking to you, young man.'

'It's all right, Kenneth. No,' she said, 'no hard feelings. I learned something, that's all.'

'What did you learn, my dear.'

'Not to go into the bushes with a boring old fart, that's what.'

'Never go anywhere with a politician, my dear,' Colonel Greenheart said. 'Kenneth, you'll be glad to know I've given Colin and Zoe my Wimsey—you know

197

the picture of the girl and the monkey—as a wedding present. Don't think young Straloch's at all pleased.'

'Must just have a word with Andrew Meldrum,' Mansie said.

'You dealt with him very nicely, my dear,' the Colonel said. 'Oh yes, I heard about your little contretemps. Of course nobody takes Mansie seriously—that's why we put him in Parliament—but you couldn't know that.'

'How's old Gavin, little Sis?'

'The poor chap's a bit low, but bearing up.'

'So you've sent Lubbock off with a flea in his ear.'

'Who told you that?'

'These things get around.'

'Well, they get around wrong. And let me tell you, you're bloody lucky from what I hear that he didn't do for you.'

'What gives you that idea? He did for me pretty thoroughly.'

'No, Andrew, he only did for your career. Not the same thing at all.'

'I might have known you'd take his side.'

'Well, natch, and it's a better side than yours.'

'Doesn't stop him from having made a balls-up, has it? These whizzkids are all the same. They always fizzle out. Comes of believing their own publicity, I suppose.'

'Whizzkids? What a frightfully old-fashioned expression. And are you going to stay in Parliament?'

Andrew turned away. He had always known how to hurt her when they had been children. He had lost the knack. There was nothing he could say about Tony which could give her pain. She stood, glad to be alone for a moment, beside Colin's absurd stuffed peacock, which had been placed in a prominent position by the bay window that overlooked the terrace, and watched Andrew cross the room to the group surrounding Ginny Prepper. She saw him take the boy Rupert by the elbow and steer him away towards the door. The boy looked back over his shoulder, opening his eyes wide, inviting the attention of anyone who might be watching, and Fiona felt her legs tremble. She longed for Tony to be there, to come through the crowd and take her away. And then she remembered the last gathering here, in this room, years ago, the day of Grace's funeral, and of how then, in a state of nervous exhaustion and depression, she had seen her mother's lover Kevin advance on her, heard him speak without listening to the precise words he uttered; and only minutes later, it seemed, had been rocking with him in a bedroom upstairs, calling for him to humiliate her, and yet savouring her revenge on Diana. It was too terrible to think of that, and she wished she didn't; but the memory wouldn't leave her. She slipped from the room, with no more than a vague acknowledgement of the greeting of friends, and climbed the stairs, and stood outside the door of that same bedroom. She listened, afraid all at once that Andrew, in some hideous parody of that earlier occasion, had brought young Rupert here; but there was silence. She pushed the door open and entered.

It was a big, cold room, north-facing, damp and still more chilly from disuse. It was dark with the shutters closed. She opened them, and looked round at the carved oak Edwardian bed, high off the floor. She laid her hand on it. Kevin had brought her nothing but shame and misery, jealousy, pain and self-contempt. Even the little triumph—no, big triumph—over her mother seemed mean and nasty. She had been afraid too: that this affair represented the first step on an avenue already trodden by Diana.

That afternoon when Tony came on her in the North British Hotel, and she had fled, in a flood of tears, denying him, she had been an entirely hollow person. If she had been the kind of girl who had breakdowns, if she didn't despise that sort of thing . . . but that was nonsense. You didn't avoid breakdowns by despising them. It was Tony who saved her. By valuing her, he taught her to value herself. And now she had turned him away. It was like Sikes and Charlie, beyond control. She saw herself dragged by necessity.

She wept when she got home from that last meeting with Tony. It needn't be the last, she told herself, but she couldn't pretend she hadn't rejected him. She accused herself of cowardice, and was only saved when she remembered the way he had accepted it, recognizing the force of what compelled her not to do what she most wanted to do.

She leaned out of the window, overlooking the darkening valley. A skein of geese flew high over the trees, heading for the firth. The air was sharp, the sky blue-black between the branches of the monkey puzzles. Music rose from the rooms below.

'Of course there must be prancing,' Colin had said. 'It wouldn't be a Scots wedding without prancing. "Merrily pranced the Quaker's wife, and merrily pranced the Quaker".'

Well, she could dance with the best of them.

Mansie, she saw on descending, had taken Straloch's girl, broad-minded of him, or indeed her, when you considered some of the things he had said about immigration.

Kenneth nuzzled Kat's ear.

'Do you remember when you asked me if I would rather you were a boy?'

'It was just a thought,' she said. 'I don't know why you keep bringing it up. It wasn't something I'd been thinking about, you know.'

'It seemed like you were.'

'Well, I wasn't, honest.'

'OK, OK, but the point is even a year ago my answer might have been different, or I wouldn't have been so sure of it, but now . . . well, look at them.'

He gestured towards Andrew and Rupert, Andrew rested his hand on Rupert's shoulder and whispered in his ear. Rupert giggled, and looked up to see his father glaring pop-eyed at him, and quite unable to pay attention to the analysis of the place of dance in Scottish culture with which Bill was gratuitously obliging him. Rupert held his father's gaze a moment, then lowered his head and hearkened to Andrew.

'He's made a mess of things, hasn't he?' Kat said.

'Andrew?'

'Yes. A pig's arse of a mess from what I've heard.'

'Oh well, we all make mistakes. I'm sorry for Andrew all the same. Colm McStay was right though. He told me Andrew had got careless.'

Jason, leaning in photogenic and practised attitude against the wall, flicked back his hair and broadened his smile as the Rev Francis Snaith-Seath proclaimed his very audible admiration for the 'truly remarkable dance' he had offered at the festival.

'I mean to say,' he said, 'it was a revelation, a real revelation. There's something of the divine in that, I said to myself, now if I could get that sort of transmission of the passionate rightness of sexuality into my sermons . . . not, you know, that I hold by sermons, not in the common meaning of the term, which belongs to the sort of church that's over and done with, the sort of church which lays down the law.' He paused and extended his hand towards Jason, then hesitated, and waved it expressively instead. 'Know what I mean? Sermons telling you what to do instead of encouraging you to explore your own personality, as you did in that dance. Do you see what I mean? So I said to myself, this is how the wonders of God can be made manifest, not that I would have you think I believe in God in the old-fashioned paternalistic sense. That's all gone out of the window. We're in a whole new ball game, sweetie, the ball game of the twenty-first century, I always say.'

'Sure,' said Jason. 'So you really liked my dance?'

'Loved it, really loved it. I mean it really showed what the church has tried to deny for two thousand years, that Jesus was gay. I mean there's no doubt about that, now, is there?'

'I guess I think of him as swinging both ways,' Jason said, flashing the perfect teeth.

Kenneth eased Kat away.

'There you are,' he said. 'See what I mean?' he quoted.

'That's nothing,' she said. 'You should hear my new supervisor. He's a born-again Gay Christian. Anyway what about Rashid?'

'Be fair. Even Rashid doesn't talk such cock. Anyway, he's given me a job, remember that. It's thanks to Rashid I could pay your fare to get you here. Besides, the mag's got potential.'

'Oh yeah? Sez who?'

'Oh all right, only quoting, only jesting. It'll do for a start . . .'

'As long's that's all it is. I don't trust Rashid.'

'Neither do I. Don't worry. Neither, to be fair, does Rashid.'

'If you say so.'

'Anyway, how's Cambridge, apart from born-again gays?'

'Dead, that's how it is. You know, they all think too much of themselves.'

'Course they do, ducky,' Colin came between them, 'there's no one else going to. Shall I tell you about dons? They are, as my friend Mr Smith of the Graham Arms says, wankers, one and all. Especially the telly dons who are always dashing up to London to show off on the box, or bore the arse off politicians.'

'They're the ones I used to admire,' Kat said.

'Well, don't. The thing about most dons is, they make even Mansie look grown-up. And in my experience the bad Cambridge dons are the worst. I know because I've lived in six countries. It's the old Puritan self-righteous, blessèd are we in the name of the Lord, who has chosen us above all other men, tradition that still lingers in the foetid fenland air.'

'When Aunty Prepper dragged me there,' Zoe said, 'my flesh literally crawled.'

*

'Liz.'

'Fiona.'

'You're looking very bonnie.'

'Well, guess what, first the Confederate-Colonel made a pass at me in the old gun-room . . .'

'That's no good,' Colin said. 'Zoe says he always loses interest half-way through.'

'Shut up, Colin, he didn't even get half-way, though I liked the way his moustache wobbled. Then Rory approached me and started talking about having a go at the pheasants.'

'And that's good?'

'Oh yes, shows he knows he's made a fool of himself and was trying to say sorry.'

'So he's coming back?'

'Well, you know we hardly have any pheasants, but it's the thought that counts. Colin, congratulations . . .'

'Happiest man in . . . Zoe, come here, slut. Liz, this is now the prudent partner of my blood—Alf, Lord T's way of describing wedded bliss. Neat, don't you think?'

'Zoe,' Fiona said, 'I didn't want to say so before the deed was done, but you're crazy to be taking my brother on. Still, perhaps you'll make a new man of him.'

'Guess I wouldn't want to do that.'

'She's only married me because of Sikes, and as for me, a gorgeous slut in cycling shorts who can see the sublime beauty of bull-terriers is an irresistible combination.'

'Honey, I hate to say it, but it looks like Aunt Ginny's winding herself up for a regular oration. I know the signs. Speak to Uncle Prepper, will you? He's the only one as can ever stop her.'

'Not so, on the contrary, I shall have no difficulty in stopping her myself.'

He advanced towards the bestseller, as Sergeant McGillicuddy approached Fiona and asked if she would strip the willow with him. She replied that she would be delighted, but her gaze was held by Colin, who had taken Ginny Prepper by the fleshy arm and was guiding her towards the dancers, where, with an imperious flick of the wrist, he summoned Mansie Niven and entrusted the lady to him.

'Isn't he just wonderful?' Zoe said. 'Isn't he cute?'

'And do you know I think she really believes that.'

They were sitting drinking tea in the kitchen, past midnight, after Kenneth had returned from putting Kat on the night train south. The dogs lay around them, and Mushtaq was curled on Fiona's lap. The clock ticked and an owl hooted deep in the woods.

'Well, he is in a way.'

'Colin?'

'Yes.'

'If you say so.'

She smiled. That was one good thing that had happened: that she could find pleasure and comfort in Kenneth's company.

'Mind if I have a drink,' he said, and went to fetch the whisky.

'Not for me'; she pushed the glass back to him. 'I'm happy with tea.'

'That chap Colm McStay, first time I met him, told me some long story about boxing. Can't remember who he was talking about, but at the end he said something like this; magnificent as war and indefensible as war. Rather like Colin, don't you think?'

'Do you know,' she said. She stroked Mushtaq, delighting in the cat's warmth. 'I think it may last.'

'Colin and Zoe?'

'Yes. She's crazy of course.'

He sipped his whisky.

'I'm glad you've made it up with Caro.'

'There seemed no point not. I was mean to her, it wasn't her fault. And Kat and you are fine?'

'Never been better. *Tant qu'il ne dure*, as Napoleon's mother used to say, when they congratulated her on one son being Emperor, and the others all Kings. Sorry, one of Colin's lines that.'

'One of Tony's too. He's got a thing about Napoleon. Poor Tony.'

Kenneth was silent. She hoped she hadn't embarrassed him, bringing Tony into the conversation. She stroked Mushtaq, whose purr sounded loud in the silence, and Kenneth lit a cigarette.

'Can I have one too, please?'

'But you don't smoke.'

'All the same . . .'

'There's the owl again,' Kenneth said. 'Strange how comforting it is.'

'If you're not a mouse.'

'Well, we're not, are we? All depends on your point of view. 'Nother of Colin's favourites. John Braine extolling the virtues of America to some parson, and the parson saying "all right if you're not black, I suppose", and Braine looks at him as if he's crazy and says "but can't you see I'm not black, you bloody fool".'

'Bit like Mansie.'

'Kat's got over it, not sure if I have.'

She drew on her cigarette, and drank some tea. It was cold, and she pushed the cup and saucer aside.

'I'd have gone with Tony if it wasn't for Charlie. Gavin being in the jug wouldn't have stopped me. It was Charlie. I couldn't take him away from here, all this. He's a right to grow up here. Do you understand?'

'Sort of. Does Tony?'

'Sort of. At least he doesn't think I'm a coward this time. But Charlie will grow up. He won't need me. Where will I be then?'

'Charlie's a good kid. So's Rosie.'

'Well, yes, but she gets on my nerves. See too much of myself in her, that's the trouble. . . .'

I'll be forty soon, she thought, and perhaps I've lost my last chance to be anything more than a mother. By sending Tony away like that, even if the terms were such that I hope to retain some kind of hold. And of course, as I've just told Kenneth, you stop being a mother in one sense, you become someone they need to be free of, and then at last you become an encumbrance, a charge, and if they're nice they pretend it's not like that, but you feel it all the same. It's good Gavin's away for the moment, she thought, even if it's not good he is where he is. But it gives us a chance to readjust, to make a start on a different something or other when he comes out. Then she pictured Tony in jail, fretting; but he might evade it. He was tough, had resources, wouldn't crumple whatever they did to him.

Kenneth said, 'You don't want to start feeling sorry for yourself.' He blushed. 'I'm speaking from experience. There's nothing so corrupting as self-pity, you know, nearly did for me. Maybe that's why Colin's come through, despite everything, because he's never succumbed to that, always been buoyant. . . .'

'Maybe,' she said.

Later, when Kenneth had gone to bed, she found she still wasn't sleepy, and opened the back door and let the dogs out into the yard. She stood by the temporary stable and listened to the breathing of the horses and the shuffle of hooves on straw. She called to the dogs and set off towards the woods and the loch.

There was a soft wind breathing damp from the south-west, but the moon was high and the clouds broken. The path before her was now clearly lit, now in shadows, but she walked with assurance. A deer broke from the undergrowth and the spaniels, defying experience, gave ever-hopeful chase. She leaned on the wooden rail of the boathouse, with the moonlight spread on the water, and listened to the night.

Later, in the afternoon, she would drive to the prison and visit Gavin. He would tell her about wood-working, and she would reply with an account of Colin's wedding, and with the good news that Maconochie had surrendered the estate papers and reduced his demands. Maconochie, they said, was heading for trouble himself, but she wouldn't report that because she knew that he would come through. The Maconochies always did. But at least the farms could now be sold and creditors pacified. With Gavin out of the way, estate business ran more smoothly, and she was working to restore order. But she wouldn't put it like that either.

As for the conditions she was going to lay down, they could wait till the old thing came out. But there would be conditions; if she had stayed for Charlie's sake, she would have a hand in the management of what would in time be Charlie's. Gavin was going to have to accept that.

That though was the easy part. Her realization this afternoon that she couldn't desert Tony made everything more difficult. She owed him something – he had made her present resolution possible. And desire went deeper than any debt. She played telephone conversations in her mind.

'It's me.'

'I knew it would be . . .'

'It'll always be me. Sometime. Somehow . . .'

She smiled. That was pure Hollywood. Could life be Hollywood? And wasn't the wish that it should be, nothing but greed? She didn't know. She had always been selfish and greedy, keeping hold of things and people. But you couldn't let go. It would ruin everything if she did . . . And yet the alternative conversation:

'It's no good. We can't ever be together. All we shall ever have is the memory of how close we came . . .'

'I can't live on memories. I've got to make a new start. If not with you, then without . . .'

Hollywood too: the Grand Renunciation scene . . .

It was no good. She would have to leave it to him. Leave it to Time.

The moon slipped behind a cloud and the water was dark below her. The dogs returned, and lay at her feet, lay around her, panting, disappointed, but never despairing. The smell of wet dog was comforting.

The owl called, from the other side of the hill now, its note caressing the night air. She heard it die away and then there was no noise but the ripple of water and rustle of leaves.

207

The Sins of the Father
ALLAN MASSIE

In Argentina during the sixties, two young people fall in love and plan to marry. But when their parents meet, Becky's blind father, a survivor of Auschwitz, recognizes the voice of Franz's father as that of a former Nazi. The ensuing war crimes trial in Israel tests the bond between Franz and Becky to the limit as they struggle to come to terms with the world their fathers made. Exploring the Holocaust's legacy and the controversial ethics of retribution. Allan Massie delivers a poignant love story and compelling drama.

'A marvellous read, dealing with big themes in an original and striking way'
Nicholas Mosley in The Daily Telegraph Books of the Year

'Has sombre intelligence rare in current fiction . . . Allan Massie treats evanescent joys and enduring terrible questions with a patient art that begins to feel like life'
The Idependent

'The ingenious and understated manner in which Massie treats the unforgotten and unforgiven makes this a tense and credible work'
The Sunday Times

'An excellent novel'
Evening Standard

'Challenges easy assumptions and skillfully explores complex moral dilemmas'
The Daily Telegraph

'This is a novel of ideas: not a twentieth-century one topped off with references to sub-atomic physics, but a nineteenth-century novel of moral ideas'
Independent on Sunday

SCEPTRE

A Question of Loyalties
ALLAN MASSIE

Winner of the Saltire Society/
Scotsman Book of the Year Award

In 1986 Etienne de Balafré pieces together the career of
the father he hardly knew who, after the fall of France
in 1940, became a prominent Vichy adherent. His quest
leads to painful discoveries, not only about the extent of
his father's collaboration and cruel death, but also about his
own life, blighted by the legacy of the past. Vividly depicting
wartime France, Allan Massie probes a morass of conflicting
loyalties and misguided ideals within a poignant, compelling
narrative.

'A brilliant novel, taking in the whole agony of Europe
leading up to its present happy state'
The Independent

'Massie has here vigorously pushed back the narrowing
boundaries of English fiction. This is a novel of scope,
substance and strength all too rare today'
The Spectator

'Massie can write like an angel'
The Sunday Telegraph

'The scope of this involving, well-peopled novel is immense,
sweeping the whole of the 20th century across Europe and
Africa. Addictively narrated through journals, confessions
and letters, the tale weaves through love, politics and
detective story on its quest for the truth. Out of one
broken man's story evolves the weighty history – and
treachery – of a whole era'
The Times

∫

SCEPTRE

Tiberius
ALLAN MASSIE

Habitually vilified as a monstrous tyrant, Emperor Tiberius has been one of history's enigmas. Now he speaks for himself – a proud, secretive, troubled man, a great general yet reluctant ruler, disgusted by the degeneracy which surrounds him. In this sequel to AUGUSTUS, Allan Massie combines a compelling study in public power and private tragedy with a vibrant portrait of the Roman world.

'Roman history provides all the political and sexual excesses of a bonkbuster plot. When it is well written and vividly characterised, as it is here, it is fascinating stuff'
The Guardian

'A fine successor to his much-acclaimed AUGUSTUS . . . as captivating an historical novel as anyone in Britain is capable of producing'
The Observer

'Confirms Allan Massie's position as one of the very best of living writers'
Literary Review

'A beautifully crafted and engrossing work of fiction'
The Scotsman

'Notable for intelligence, fluid and fascinating narrative, balanced judgement, serious speculation in serious matters'
The Daily Telegraph

'Massie is at his most mature. He knows his way round Rome like a blind beggar, and he has its history etched on his cuff . . . hypnotic'
Scotland on Sunday

'Fascinating and intriguing. Massie dramatizes the actual process by which history is made'
The Glasgow Herald

SCEPTRE

Caesar
ALLAN MASSIE

Allan Massie's Caesar is a perception of greatness overreaching itself. Through the eyes of one of his comrades, Decimus Brutus, we observe Caesar the enchanter, the showman, the general whose soldiers will follow him anywhere, while their wives supply his bed. We see the man of authority whose charm can be devastating but whose emotional engagement is nil. In his third Roman novel after TIBERIUS and AUGUSTUS, Allan Massie writes with a wry wit about human frailty, while political philosophy has never been clothed in such an atmosphere of highly charged sexuality.

'His Roman novels, this one included, are full of vital, complex characters dug up out of the ancient historians and given new life'
The Sunday Times

'In his third Roman novel, Allan Massie's Muse sings a seductive song of Caesar, sex and civil war. The combination makes for entertaining reading'
Times Literary Supplement

'Caesar has no real sense of the past, no sympathy with the way others may think, no sensitivity to immemorial affections . . . Massie in every respect, is the opposite to this Caesar'
The Independent

'To take the conspiracy against Julius Caesar . . . and make of it something fresh and exciting is no mean feat. This is what Allan Massie has done in this fine novel'
Evening Standard

'The flavour of the period is recaptured in a series of clever touches which manage to be convincing while, at the same time, connecting with the way we live today'
The Sunday Telegraph

SCEPTRE